NO EARTHLY BOUNDARIES

by Rosemary Smith

PORTLAND • OREGON
INKWATERPRESS.COM

Publisher: Inkwater Press | www.inkwaterpress.com

Paperback
ISBN-13 978-1-59299-658-2 | ISBN-10 1-59299-658-2

Kindle
ISBN-13 978-1-59299-659-9 | ISBN-10 1-59299-659-0

Printed in the U.S.A.
All paper is acid free and meets all ANSI standards for archival quality paper.

1 3 5 7 9 10 8 6 4 2

DEDICATION

I dedicate this book to my husband, LTC (Retired) Clarence A. Smith, III. I could never have written it without him. I do love that man.

ACKNOWLEDGMENTS

I would like to thank all of my friends for listening to my thoughts and allowing me to use them as guinea pigs for this book. When you looked at the ceiling and rolled your eyes, I knew that I was on a wrong tack. Thank you, My dear husband, for reading every new twist and turn in the story and my Pokeno group for not throwing me out of the game every time I thought of something new that I had to discuss. Thank you, Sean Jones and all the staff at Inkwater Press for all your help and encouragement. Thank you, Linda Franklin, my editor, for pointing out that I probably didn't need to use the word "really" thirty-nine times in this one manuscript and for being patient with my efforts to make it as good as it could be. You gave me the courage to finally declare it done, even if my finger did shake as I hit the send button on the sign-off e-mail. I hope that all of you enjoy the story.

CHAPTER ONE

In September of 1945, after more than three years of fighting in WWII and recovering from his injuries and finally processing out of the Army in New York, Jean Marc Thibodaux bought himself a ticket for a southbound Greyhound bus. He packed all his belongings into a shabby olive drab duffel bag and climbed on board. The big bus ate up the miles as he slept sitting upright in the hard seat, propped against the window with his jacket rolled up for a pillow. He changed buses several times and ate stale white bread sandwiches and drank bad coffee in more small towns along the way than he would have ever guessed existed. The closer he got to his destination, the more excited he became. After counting his nickels and dimes, he used a pay phone in Alabama to call the General Store in Butte La Rose, Louisiana, to let his family know that he was on his way home. His best friend's father, Tom Landry, answered his ring and told him that he would gladly pass the word that their own local soldier boy was coming back home.

If Mr. Landry thought there was anything strange about the boy asking him to tell Amy that he loved her, he didn't say anything. He was not sure which Amy the boy was referring to, so he would keep that part to himself and let the boy do his own romancing when he arrived. The only Amy that he would have associated with Jean Marc Thibodaux was Amy Benoit and she was now married to someone else and expecting a child, so he felt certain that she couldn't be the Amy the boy was talking about.

Jean Marc leaned his head back and stared out the window of the moving bus. A lot of country had gone by that window over the past few days. He'd been cold when the journey started and now the weather was hot and his butt was getting sore from sitting in the same position on the hard seat. His long legs were cramping and he had a deep ache in the one that was injured during the war. Since the bus wasn't crowded, he had a seat to himself and was able to prop his bad leg up when it hurt too badly. It hung off the seat into the aisle, so he did have to be watchful, in case one of the rowdy little kids ran past, but the worst offenders were sleeping in their seats beside their mama, so he stuck it out there for a short time to ease the pain. Using his last match to light up a cigarette, he closed his eyes, breathing deeply and taking in as much of the smoke as possible. He needed the nicotine fix to calm his jangled nerves. He could feel every bump and dip in the road and the vibrations shook his tired body as the vehicle turned off the blacktop and onto an even narrower corduroy road that led to home. His feet knew this road. He had walked it barefooted a thousand times as a child. The trees were covered with dust and the road was full of holes, but it didn't matter. The sun was setting and it was beautiful and he was almost home.

He pointed to the bright flash of silver in the sky and said aloud, "A wishing star to welcome me back...that's good. I'll take all the wishes I can get." The lady across from him smiled and nodded. She was headed to Texas and had a long ride ahead of her. She looked like she could use a few wishes of her own.

The star was brighter than the ones he remembered and seemed to head straight for the ground, but he dismissed the oddity and kept on with his thoughts.

"I do have a lot to wish for and to be grateful for," he said to himself.

He closed his eyes again and said a silent prayer and loosely made the sign of the cross, while hoping no one would notice. He had spent most of his twenty-five years in his own Catholic area, and when he left home to go to basic training, he discovered that the whole world was not Catholic after all and he began to be a little more reserved about showing his faith.

CHAPTER TWO

After surviving the injuries he got fighting in the foxholes of France and the long stay in the hospital with several painful surgeries to repair his damaged leg, he was within spitting distance from the place he loved more than any other place on earth. It might not look like much to other folks, but to Jean Marc Thibodaux, it was as close to heaven as he wanted to get for a few more years.

During the long hours in his hospital bed, he had made a plan. Now he was checking off the items as he accomplished each one.

Item number one was to recover from his injuries. The healing was finished and all that was left was a dull ache and the small limp in his gait that would probably be there for the rest of his days. He wasn't bothered by the limp very much. He was thankful that the doctors had saved his damaged leg and he was glad to be able to walk at all. He did wonder if Amy would be concerned about it, but he would be able to do all the things he used to do, so he didn't think of it as a disability.

The second thing was to get home and that was almost accomplished too. He could already see the bright light shining down from the creosote pole beside the road that ran in front of Landry's General Store. The bus ride from New York City to Butte La Rose was long and uncomfortable, but he would have walked, if that had been the only way. He had even considered sticking out his thumb and hitch-hiking to save the money, but changed his mind when he realized that could take weeks to do and he had been away long enough already.

The next big thing was to marry his precious Amy. He expected to accomplish that one as soon as he had a talk with her papa and they made the arrangements. She had not written to him in a while, but she never was a big letter writer and Jean Marc was sure that everything would be all right once they were together again. *Love conquers all* was more than an old saying. He believed it. He'd been in love with Amy Benoit since he was fifteen years old and was convinced that she was his and always would be. Whatever problem caused her to stop writing would melt away as soon as they felt their arms around each other and tasted that first kiss.

The fourth thing on his list was to get his traps and fishing lines set out again and make enough money from fishing and furs to buy an automobile. He spent hours debating with himself about whether to get a car or a truck and had decided that if he got the right car, he could fit everything he needed in the trunk. Everyone he knew in Butte La Rose owned trucks when he left and he wanted to be the first in his family and maybe in the whole village to own a family car. It would take a little time, but he was ready to begin saving. He figured that if Amy saved her butter and egg money and he did well with his trapping, it would not take too long. He knew that Amy and her mama sold their extra butter and eggs to Mr. Landry at the store. Amy could most likely continue to do that after they were married. They would get a cow and some chickens and let Mama Nature take her course and before very long they would be riding around town in a new Packard or maybe a new DeSoto. They'd have fun driving them all and choosing the one they liked the best.

Yep, he thought, Butte La Rose was not exactly a booming metropolis. Life there had probably changed very little over the past few years. Jean Marc fully expected to go home and slip back into the life he left over three years ago like a well-worn flannel shirt and all the bad thoughts about things that had happened to him over the past few years would go away and everything would be good again. He had dreamed about it for the last year. Yep. He had a plan and so far, it was all happening exactly the way he had hoped.

CHAPTER THREE

Jean Marc leaned forward, propping his elbows on the back of the empty seat in front of him and looked past the driver and out the front windshield. He saw a group of people waiting under the light at Mr. Landry's store. No doubt at least some of them were there to welcome him home. He grinned. It made his heart beat a little faster just to think of it. Amy would be in his arms in only a few more minutes.

When the air brakes on the bus wheezed to a halt, he looked at all the faces. His mama and papa were there, along with his older brother Aaron and his wife, Patrice, and their two kids. Mr. and Mrs. Landry were there. His two best friends, Boo Landry and Elloi Comeaux, were jumping up and down on the side of the road like oversized twelve-year-old boys, trying to see him before he stood up in his seat. They were grinning from ear to ear. Watching them bounce made him smile too. He didn't see Amy but decided that she must be inside the store and coming out to surprise him in a minute. He watched the doorway to see her face.

The bus driver stood up and gave his little speech about the bus leaving in exactly thirty minutes and for them to get out and stretch their legs if they wanted to, but not to be late or he would leave without them. It was the same tired speech that he gave at every stop and nobody paid much attention after they heard it a time or two. Jean Marc was glad that he was not going to have to hear it again. The people stood up and gathered their sacks and kids and shuffled to the door to step out one by one.

The driver opened up the luggage compartment in the bottom of the bus and took Jean Marc's big olive green duffel bag out for him. Boo grabbed it up and tossed it into the back of his own truck for the ride home.

Jean Marc's mama nearly pulled him off the bottom step trying to give him a hug. His papa and brother and Boo and Elloi were pumping his hands and hitting him on the back and doing all those things that men do to show affection for each other without admitting to it. He hugged Patrice and bent down to say hello to his two young nieces, but they dug their bare toes in the sand and hid their faces in Patrice's skirts, peeking out at him with big brown eyes and shy smiles. The older one had been a baby when he left and the younger one had not even been born. *Maybe a few things had changed while he was away, after all,* he thought. But those changes were good ones and he could accept them easily.

"Where is Amy? I was hoping that Amy was going to be here," he said, letting his disappointment show in his voice and on his face as he looked around at the faces that looked back at him.

The group fell silent and his parents both looked red and embarrassed and stumbled over their words and then stepped back. No one seemed to have the courage to answer.

Jean Marc frowned and asked again, "What's going on here, Mama, Papa? Where is she? Is she all right? Why isn't she here to meet me?"

Aaron was the one who finally said the words. "Amy isn't coming, Brother. She married Pierre Autement last June and they are having a baby now." After dropping his verbal bombshell, Aaron took a big step back as if he were afraid of what would happen next. He needn't have been worried. Jean Marc was not capable of doing him any harm at that point.

"Married? To Pierre?" Jean Marc stammered.

It felt as though he had been punched in the gut. His ears started ringing and his insides churned and he broke into a cold sweat. His knees felt weak all of a sudden and he reached out one hand to lean on Elloi's big arm to steady himself. Then he bent over to hold onto his knees and very nearly emptied his last baloney sandwich onto the gravel of the parking lot right there in front of all of them. He wasn't prepared for that kind of news.

Jumbled thoughts buzzed around like bees inside his head. *Yeah, she had stopped writing, but before that, she hadn't said anything about seeing anyone else. Pierre was supposed to be watching out for her, but she had never shown any of that kind of interest in him. I wouldn't have asked him to watch out for her if I had ever seen any spark between the two of them.* Jean Marc wanted to believe in their love so much that he had held on, in spite of her not writing. He looked up at them all standing there watching him and saw the pity in their faces. He didn't want their damned pity. He wanted Amy. But Amy wasn't there. It hurt bad. It hurt him worse than any pain he had felt in a long time.

He silently prayed, "Oh Jesus and Mother Mary, please don't let me cry," as he felt his eyes filling up in spite of his efforts to stop it. Here he was, a grown man who went off to war and came home and ended up crying like a baby over a girl. He tried to mentally grab himself up and make himself strong again before he humiliated himself totally.

His mama grabbed his arm and told him, "Come on now, Jean Marc, we can talk about that later, son, we're just glad to have you back home. We've got us a chicken and sausage gumbo and some fried rabbit and greens and I even made you a syrup cake, so let's get you home, where you belong and feed you some of your mama's home cookin'. We'll talk about that other stuff later. OK?" She began to lead him toward the truck. He welcomed the distraction and support and stood up straight, took a deep cleansing breath, and reached out to help her climb up onto the seat of Papa's old truck.

CHAPTER FOUR

Amy was married to Pierre. He felt weak again, thinking about it.

Mr. and Mrs. Landry had to go back inside the store to wait on the other people who had gotten off the bus. There were cold drinks and coffee and hot *boudin* to sell as well as the usual candy bars and sandwiches. The rest of the welcoming committee loaded into their trucks and headed off down the dirt road in a convoy toward the Thibodaux's place. Boo and Elloi tagged along without an invitation, but Jean Marc's mama, Laurine, had fed those two boys so many times over the years that she didn't even think about it being anything unusual. They felt like two more of her own and that is the way she had always treated them. They might be handy to have around if the subject of Amy Benoit, well, better make that Amy Autement now, came up and it was going to come up pretty quick, if she knew her son. She'd been dreading that conversation all day. It was going to be hard. He was hurting bad and they did have some explaining to do. She had her reasons for not telling him when Amy and Pierre got married and she would have to be the one to tell him the whole story, and was not looking forward to it at all. The ride home was short, so there was not much time for conversation in the truck. Jean Marc was not up to conversation at that point anyway. She reached over and patted his leg several times. Even with the bad stuff, it was good to have her boy home again.

The dinner table was crowded. Every extra chair and stool had been pressed into service. The platters and bowls were full to heaping. The food was simple and mostly made from things they caught or grew or shot themselves. But the loving touch that was added by the cook was enough to make it taste better to Jean Marc than anything he had tasted in over three years. He savored every bite and praised his mama's skill in the kitchen. She grinned and soaked up the praise along with the gravy. It made her feel good to see them all together again under her roof and enjoying her food.

They each seemed to have a million questions for Jean Marc about what he had seen and what he had done and he did his best to answer them. He had been farther away from home than most of the people in the whole town had ever been. He had seen Paris and the little town in France where his own ancestors had come from. He understood that they would have a lot of questions. He had only one question and it hung there, floating in the air around them like a big black rain cloud.

Finally, when he could stand it no longer, he waited for a break in the conversations and timidly asked, "Which one of you is going to tell me about Amy?"

Patrice got very busy cutting up a piece of rabbit meat for her older daughter and the men all looked at the flow-ered tablecloth and got red-faced and quiet and began to pick at the food on their plates. His mama took a deep shaky breath and began to twist her apron into a knot in her lap as she began to speak.

"*Mais-la*, I guess that would be me. OK. Here it is... This is the thing. Son, you remember when you left, you told Pierre to watch out for Amy for you while you were away? Well, he did exactly what you said. He was with her almost every day, watching and taking care of her, just like you told him. *Mais*, after a while, I guess Amy began to see that you were gone and Pierre was close by. The more time they spent together, the closer they got. She told me one day that she was finding it hard to write love letters to you and still see Pierre every day and that she was going to tell you that she and Pierre were thinking seriously about getting married. Son, I told her not to tell you that. I told her. So, you can blame all this on me. You needed that hope of coming home to Amy to get you through that war. I was afraid that if she took that little bit of hope away from you that you would have nothing to hold onto and that you might get hurt or killed. So, I told her that it was better to not say anything about that and wait until you came home and then we'd handle the telling for her. When you got hurt, you still needed that dream to get you through all those surgeries and other stuff that you went through. We couldn't be with you over there and I didn't know what to do." She wiped her tears away with the tail of her apron and shook her head. "Poo-yieee!" she said. "So, I still didn't tell you. Now...it is done and you are home, thanks be to Jesus. And I guess you can blame your own mama for breaking your heart. I told the girl to go on and do what she felt and to marry the man she loves. She and Pierre are doing fine.

They were meant to be together, Jean Marc, you can see it in the way they are with each other. And you are going do fine too. She was not the right girl for you, son. I knew that from the very beginning when the two of you were just kids. If she had been the right one, then none of this would have happened. You know that, yeah? There's somebody else out there waiting for you and now that you are free then you can go out and find her. Amy Benoit plainly wasn't the one, that's all there is to it. You are going to see that's true, son, you'll see."

The men at the table were still silent, and watching Jean Marc's every move. After a few seconds, he blinked back the tears and pushed his chair back and walked around the end of the table to his mama and pulled her up to give her a big hug. The tears were streaming down her face and she was hurting as badly as he was. He planted a kiss on the top of her head, which didn't even come up to his chin, and told her, "Mama, I am not good at saying the mushy stuff, but I love you and I know that you did the right thing. You were right. I was holding onto that dream. I needed it to live. I just have to figure out what to do with myself now that the dream is not going to happen." They rocked from side to side and hugged.

Jean Marc stopped the rocking suddenly and said, "There is one thing that might make me feel a little better. I want me a big piece of that syrup cake you mentioned and a refill on my coffee." He gave her another kiss and then offered her his handkerchief to wipe her eyes. She used it to wipe her face and then blew her nose in it and tucked it into the pocket of her apron to put in the wash. She also swatted him on the behind because that is what mamas do. They both laughed. Everybody around the table looked relieved and began to laugh with them.

They all breathed easier and the talking began again with everybody trying to talk at the same time. The cake was served up and the coffee cups refilled and Jean Marc tucked away his bad feelings for later when he was alone and could take them out and examine each one of them more closely.

A certain darker inside part of him wanted to find Pierre Autement and break every bone in his scrawny little body. Another part of him wanted to confront Amy and find out why she had been unfaithful and why she preferred Pierre over him. She had said that she loved him and would wait for him no matter how long he was gone. Well, now that he thought of it seriously, what she said was that she would TRY to wait for him. A man hears what he wants to hear, sometimes. After that little reality check, he decided that he would think about all that later. For now, he was enjoying the flavors of home and being surrounded by loved ones. That would do for tonight.

CHAPTER FIVE

After supper, they sat around talking until nearly bedtime and then Jean Marc went out onto the front porch and climbed the ladder up into the loft or *garçonniere* where he had slept with his brother Aaron when they were younger. He fumbled a bit until he reached the lamp on the table and scratched a match to light it. The room looked the same as it always had. It made him smile. The two twin sized beds were neatly made and beside each was a braided rag rug lovingly made by their mama to keep warm feet from the cold floor in the winter time. Each of the boys had made his side of the room his own.

Aaron's side still had his first big winning poker hand thumb-tacked to the rough boards of the wall by his bed. The cards were yellowed and curled now. He used to brag that he had won over fifty dollars with that hand, which was not bad when one considered that he had only been thirteen years old at the time. The next day, he had gotten a taste of the razor strop from his papa and had to return the money to his papa's friends who had lost it to him the previous night. The grown men claimed they only lost because they'd had a few too many sips from the jug of homemade whiskey in the back of Mr. Landry's store. They claimed that they were trying to be nice to the kid by letting him play at all and he must have cheated some way, but none of them knew how. He and Aaron had talked about that night at the supper table only a few hours before.

Papa said, "Aaron, you remind me of Uncle Antoine. You need to watch yourself, so you don't end up dead from a knife fight over a poker game the way Uncle Antoine did."

Aaron replied, "Papa, I am smart enough not to end up that way. Uncle Antoine drank as much when he was gambling as the others in the game. I learned at a tender age that I had to keep my head clear, even if the others drank themselves stupid. Gambling is my job. So, I drink very little while I am at work. You remember that whipping you gave me when I was thirteen years old?"

Papa laughed and nodded his head. He said, " Oh yeah, I do, Aaron, that was when I knew how good you were at your job. I couldn't believe you had outdone that bunch. I was secretly proud of you but caught between a rock and a hard place."

He looked at us all at the table and pointed at Aaron and said, "Listen, yeah, he had taken money from Cecil LeBoeff, who was known throughout the area to be the best poker player in the parish. Those guys were serious gamblers and they couldn't let it get out, that they had lost to a thirteen-year-old kid. I knew he hadn't cheated, but there was no way I could have let on. I had to whoop his butt to save my own face with my friends."

Aaron said, "I learned that trick about not drinking from watching Cecil. Cecil would sip and pretend to get drunk but was usually the most sober player at the table. Knowing that I had beat Cecil and got more than fifty bucks on that game was when I knew I would be able to make a living as a gambling man. It was worth getting my butt whipped."

Papa wasn't pleased by knowing his son was bitten by the gambling bug and always hoped that things would change one day. He felt like Aaron was too smart to make his living like that. So far, Papa was still waiting and Mama refused to discuss it. Whenever gambling came up in conversation, she invariably tried to change the subject as quickly as possible.

There was also a picture of a fighting-rooster that had been torn out of a magazine hanging above the bed. It was a prize-winning bird and Aaron said one day he would have a dozen of that kind. Now, he likely had more than a dozen of the best chickens he could find around. Jean Marc repeatedly said that his brother Aaron was a gambling fool. He would bet on which blade of grass grew the fastest. But, he seemed to make a good living at it, and he and his family did OK.

His wife, Patrice, also did not approve, and prayed for him constantly, hoping that her prayers would be enough to save his gambling soul. The strange part was that even though she disapproved of his gambling, she had complete faith in his ability to provide for their family. He brought home the winnings and she kept out enough to cover their expenses and gave him back the rest to use in his gambling endeavors. The odd arrangement worked for them and Jean Marc reckoned that it wasn't anybody else's business anyway. After six years of marriage, they seemed happy and the children were beautiful. Jean Marc wanted a wife and children of his own one day.

His own side of the room had not changed since he stayed there the last night before he left for basic training. It had a shelf that was filled with books and that last night he had tacked a map of the world on the wall above his bed. He had circled in pencil all the places that he wanted to visit. There were a lot of circles. One day, he would take another pencil and put an X through the places that he had seen with his own eyes. Maybe, if he could get hold of a pencil, he would do that tomorrow. It would be fun to see the changes on the map. He blew out the kerosene lamp and slid into his old bed and thought of how comfortable it was. It was a lot better than the hard seat of that Greyhound bus. The best part was that it was home. He was asleep before he had time to think anymore.

CHAPTER SIX

The sleek silver craft descended rapidly as the pilot searched for a stable bit of ground to use as a landing spot. His aircraft was built for rapid travel through open space and was not well suited for landings on the wet and uneven ground of the swamp.

Sacam, the explorer, unloaded his empty boxes and containers and began to search the surrounding area for the flora and fauna that he needed to collect and catalog. He had been here many times. Each time, he took careful notes of surrounding conditions and what plants and other creatures grew in the area where each specimen was located.

He wiped his pale hand across his bald head and marveled once again at this wonderful place. He had visited many different locations on this planet, but this one had perpetually fascinated him. There was enough work to be done in this one section to keep him busy for months.

C

The next few days were a blur of activity for Jean Marc. He went over to his own place and opened up the doors and windows to let it begin to air out. The critters had taken up residence while he was gone and he had a lot of sweeping and cleaning to do to make it ready for him to live in again. He threw out a lot of things that had been ruined by the heat, humidity, and mold and mildew in the closed-up house. He checked over the wood-burning stove and flue to see that it was safe to use and fired it up to make himself a pot of coffee. He drank from the big white cup that Papaw had used and felt better by doing it. He was on the right track now and was ready to face whatever he had to face.

The only thing that made sense to him was to jump back into life with both feet. OK. One part of the plan had not worked out but the rest of it could still happen the way he planned. Work would make it better. It always did before and would most likely put things in order for him again. He would get the house cleaned out and move back in as soon as possible. He didn't want to stay at his parents' any longer than he had to. It was extra work for them and Jean Marc had spent enough time already in the Army with people around him and watching every move that he made. Hanging on to the past was not going to help anybody either. It was time to move on. He felt good about it.

Jean Marc's tiny cypress-wood house, set up high on sturdy marine pilings, had belonged to his grandfather. Papaw's own father had built it by hand over fifty years before Jean Marc was even born. It was rustic and without many graces but was sturdy and would outlast them all unless it got blown away in a hurricane. It had survived a few of those already so there didn't seem to be much to worry about. The old house was strong and full of good memories. Before he passed, Papaw had installed electric wiring and indoor plumbing, so it was more modern than a lot of the houses in Butte La Rose.

Jean Marc had moved in to help his grandfather while

still a teenaged boy. The old man seemed healthy enough, but liked having the company and Jean Marc liked being there to chop wood or help with the garden. It made him feel useful and needed. It had proven to be a good arrangement for them both. He learned a lot of common sense from his papaw during those years and his grandfather's sudden death from a stroke left an empty hole in the young man's life. Papaw left him the house in his handwritten will.

After his grandfather's death, things had gotten confusing for Jean Marc. He was old enough to marry and he certainly wanted to marry Amy Benoit eventually, but something was holding him back. He continued to work his traps and hunt and fish, as he had done since he was old enough, but listening to the news on the radio, especially the parts about the war raging in Europe and the bombing of Pearl Harbor, had made Jean Marc feel the need to make changes in his life. His small community was no longer big enough to hold his restless spirit. He felt useless since Papaw was gone. He needed more direction and a bigger purpose. The US Government called for volunteers and he felt the call personally. And so he drove Papaw's truck to Baton Rouge one day and signed on the dotted line. Nobody in the family was happy about his decision. In fact, he and Aaron almost came to blows at the supper table that first night after he told them all what he had done. Papa was not sure he had done the right thing and Mama was silent and scared but Aaron was downright angry. He insisted that it had been a stupid thing to do and it would cause problems for everybody in the village. Jean Marc hadn't understood how his joining the Army could cause a problem for anybody except himself. He felt it was nobody's business but his own. He was a grown man and could make his own decisions. It had put a strain on the relationship with his brother right up 'til the day he left.

A few nights later after supper at his girlfriend's house, he and Amy sat on her porch holding hands.

He asked her, "You will wait for me until I get back and then we are going to get married, right?"

She picked at her cuticle and answered quietly, "I will try to wait for you, Jean Marc, but I don't understand why you have to go. You say all that stuff about the Nazis and the Japanese but my papa says that is all crap. He says those people from over there are not going to come here to fight with us and we don't have any business going over there and getting involved in their messes."

He held her close and kissed her and told her, "Ohh, *Sha*, I don't want to leave you. You know that. But your papa is wrong about saying they wouldn't come here. They already did come here and that is part of why I have to go, Amy. I have to go because I do love you."

She sniffed away the tears and begged, "I don't understand all that stuff. All I know is that I don't want you to go. If you stay here, we can get married this next summer. I'd rather see that happen than for me to be sitting here by myself waiting and being scared that you would get shot or blown up or something. Please don't go. If you really love me then you won't go off and leave me. Please stay here."

Then she began to give him some very tender persuasion that certainly gave him things to remember while he was away.

Evidently, she didn't know about or remember the Japanese raid on Pearl Harbor or didn't understand that meant that the enemy had already come to our own shores to wage war. Maybe that should've been his first clue that things weren't exactly right for the two of them.

Her parents were against his going away too. They didn't listen to the radio or read the newspapers the way that Jean Marc's family did and were not as aware of things going on in the world. Amy was confused. If she had been the right girl, then maybe she and her parents would have supported his decision and understood his reasons for going to do his part.

But then, sometimes, he wasn't sure that he truly understood all the reasons that made him do the things he did, so how could he have expected a girl of nineteen, who had never been farther from home than Baton Rouge, to understand it any better than he did? It had been a long and painful journey, both physically and emotionally, and he had learned a lot, including the fact that answering a call can be costly.

CHAPTER SEVEN

That next afternoon, Jean Marc pulled out all the traps that he had stored before going away. Before he left for the war, he had routinely set out his metal spring traps in the swampy areas around the Atchafalaya basin and then skinned the fur-bearing animals that were caught and sold the hides for money. He wanted to get the traps out as soon as possible and start up his business again. His old yellow dog, Chili, followed every step as he worked. He sorted through the traps so that he could count them and figure out how many he would need to replace or repair. Over the time he'd been gone, some of them had been moved from where he had put them. He found some of the older traps in the outside storage shed, but they were rusted and needed a lot of work. He sanded and brushed and cleaned them all afternoon to put them in good enough condition to be of any use. His papa gave him some of his own that he wasn't using anymore and then Aaron showed up with some he had taken as partial payment for a gambling debt that a guy owed to him on a rooster fight. That gave him enough to get started and he made up his mind to go out the very next day to set the traps and take a look around to see how much the swamp had changed since he had been away from home. After he sold his first load of furs, he could buy more traps.

There was talk about the basin flooding and changes in

the water flow and he wanted to see the changes for himself. The government had opened up some flood gates after a big flood up north and the locals said the extra water coming down was drowning out whole villages. They also complained that it was bringing down silt that was filling up the river, making it muddy and ruining the fishing. The chemical fertilizer washing into the water from farms up north was also causing an overgrowth of algae and plant life in the water of the bayou. The water hyacinths were floating rafts of roots and vegetation that tore up boat motors and made fishing impossible in some areas. Added to the confusion was talk of the wildcat oil companies coming in to explore for oil. The locals were very much against that. The loggers had come in years before and divided the area with deep canals and cut down virtually all the old cypress timber, and those two things had caused a big part of the current flooding problems, so they were not anxious for another big industry to come along and do more damage. The life in and around the swamp was changing more perhaps than Jean Marc had expected. The salt water was coming even farther up into the canals during high tide and mixing with the fresh water and changing the kinds of fish available to catch for food as well as to sell. It was affecting all of their livelihoods. Some of the locals were so discouraged that they were moving out of the swamp and going to bigger towns to find different kinds of work. Jean Marc could not imagine doing that. The coffee can that held his money might be nearly empty right now, but he was determined to fill it up again and was not ready to even think about leaving home any time soon.

CHAPTER EIGHT

After a simple supper in his own house, he sat outside at the edge of the water and soaked up the idea of being home. He leaned backwards in his homemade wooden chair, looking out over the murky waters of the basin. By the calendar, it was autumn, but it was still warm even with the sun well below the tree tops. He closed his dark eyes and ran his hands through his straight black hair and listened to the sounds of nature that surrounded him and slapped at a mosquito without even thinking about it. Warm sweat slowly trickled down his back and neck beneath his loose-fitting white shirt and cleaned the toxins from his body from the inside out. If only there was a way to clean the bad thoughts from his mind as easily.

The night birds called to each other and the old alligator who lived around the bend grunted as he did every evening about this time. Ordinary sounds were soothing on this lonely night. Jean Marc felt the need to be outside, soaking up the sounds and odors and feelings of this place he called home. Being alone in his own place also gave him the chance to take out some of those bothersome thoughts and deal with them in his own way.

He rubbed the ache in his bad leg and thought of the night he was hurt. Sometimes, it played like a moving picture inside his head. He could see it so clearly that it was like being at the picture show, except that the events were real and had happened to him and they were not good memories. He wished that he could make his mind stop the constant replay. He lit up a hand-rolled cigarette and leaned forward, blowing the smoke out of his nostrils and propping his elbows on his knees. He let the images play uninterrupted this once. Maybe it would be enough to make them go away for a while.

Shortly before the end of the war, in a foxhole somewhere in France, four guys, including two good ole boys from Alabama and Jean Marc and Eric, a newly found friend from a small town in Pennsylvania, were discussing the differences in what they called their normal lives. They laughed about the similarities in their families, even with the huge differences in their heritage. They talked about their favorite foods. Eric's family was fond of potatoes and beer. Jean Marc told them about hunting the ducks and deer in Louisiana. They compared their crazy aunts and uncles and described their pretty girl cousins in great detail. Eric admitted that he had some problems dealing with the fact that his family background was German and here they were fighting the Germans. He was afraid that he might be killing his own not very distant relatives. It was a point to consider but neither Jean Marc nor the other boys had an answer to their friend's dilemma. None of the others had those issues although they tried to understand for Eric's sake.

Eric and Jean Marc also discovered that they were both Catholic. The two young men found that they had a lot more in common than they ever would have imagined, considering the distance between their homes and the differences in their heritage. They finally concluded that large Catholic families would be likely to have a lot in common, no matter where they lived. Both of them took comfort in that notion and prayed together often. It helped when the exploding shells were falling all around them and bullets were whistling through the night. They went to mass together whenever they got the chance. Once, there was a priest who came to them in their foxhole one day, announcing, "Any Catholics in here?" The backsliding Baptist boys from Alabama sat in their corners and watched as the Catholics prayed together and took Holy Communion. Jean Marc had included them in his prayers, whether they had asked for it or not. In war times, they could all use a blessing and a prayer no matter what religion they practiced.

The big guns had been firing all evening but had been aimed farther south from where Jean Marc and Eric and the other two guys were hunkered down in the mud. They had foolishly begun to think that they would not see any action at all that night. The four of them shared their evening meal, swapping cans and enjoying the chocolate bars and cigarettes from their rations. They even spent some time enlarging their space, to give each of them a little more elbow room.

The three German soldiers who jumped down into their foxhole caught them all completely by surprise. They fought with their attackers hand to hand and one of the boys from Alabama managed to eliminate one of them with his knife and the other two jumped out of the hole again and ran back into the night. It happened very quickly and left them all in a kind of shock.

Up close and personal...the kind of fighting that gave a soldier bad dreams if he was the sensitive type or made him harden up inside, if he was able to tune it out. Jean Marc and his three buddies looked at the face of the dead German soldier and then looked back at each other. It made their situation become very real and all were grateful that it was not one of them lying there dead in that puddle.

The grenade came flying out of nowhere over their heads and landed with a splat in the mud beside the dead German. Jean Marc and Eric stared down at it for a fraction of a second and knew that this was a life-altering moment for both of them since they were the ones in the center of the foxhole and closest to the grenade.

Jean Marc yelled, "Grenade!" at the top of his lungs and dove away from the deadly bomb as he had been taught to do in basic training.

His new friend Eric threw himself on top of the thing just as it exploded. It was a selfless act, but they did not teach that in basic. Without a doubt, he saved Jean Marc's life and possibly the lives of the two other young men on either side of them in the foxhole. Jean Marc had felt the impact of something hitting his legs, but lay there for a heartbeat, blinking and wondering if he truly wanted to see what had happened to his friend in the hole beside him. He heard a moan and looked back to see Eric lying face down across the body of the dead German. He pushed, pulled and dragged himself for the short distance to get over to him and rolled him over into his own lap.

"Eric, buddy, you all right?" he asked as he looked at his friend and immediately realized that his friend was definitely not all right. The young man had taken the biggest part of the grenade's impact to his midsection and was not all right at all.

Jean Marc rocked his body back and forth and muttered over and over, *"Mon cher comrade,"* with tears running down his face. The two boys from Alabama leaned back against the walls of dirt and thanked God for their survival.

Eric looked up at Jean Marc with big questions in his blue eyes and died without saying a word.

Jean Marc had already called for a medic, but now he yelled again as loud as he could. There he sat, in the bottom of a muddy hole with a dead comrade draped across his lap and a dead German soldier beside them both. The bad part was that except for their uniforms Eric and the dead German looked like brothers.

That bothered Jean Marc a lot. He made the sign of the cross and prayed for his friend and for the German too, who had been a soldier, exactly like them, following orders and hoping to survive.

After what seemed like an eternity, the medical team arrived. They roughly lifted Eric's body off Jean Marc's lap and placed what was left of him on a stretcher. Two other guys carted him off. It was awful to see him like that. He thought of the boy's relatives in Pennsylvania and wished that he had the address so that he could write them a letter to tell them about the heroic, but stupid thing that Eric had done. They deserved to know that Eric had been a hero. They deserved to know that his last few hours had been spent thinking and talking about them at home. He had wondered about the girl back in Pennsylvania, who, according to Eric, was planning a wedding. In one brief moment...less than a moment...the whole world was different for all of them. At that point in time, he could not help but see his own sweet Amy's face in his mind and wonder what she would do if the same thing happened to him. Would her heart be broken? How would her life be different with him gone? Who would she marry if he did not return home? It had been a scary thought.

CHAPTER NINE

After they took Eric away, the medics began to gently examine Jean Marc. Other than the loud ringing in his ears, caused by his close proximity to the explosion of the grenade, he had not even realized that he had injuries of his own. One leg was badly broken in several places, with bits of bone and shrapnel sticking out of what was left of his uniform pants. The other leg was damaged but not as severely. He had other cuts and bruises that needed attention, but his legs took the worst of it. The medics gave his a shot of something for pain and then carefully lifted him onto another stretcher and carried him away. He closed his eyes and immediately saw the last scene of Eric's life playing like a movie inside his head for the first time. A tear slid down the side of his face and landed on the canvas stretcher as they bounced and jostled him into the back of a big truck that would take him to the hospital.

He thought, *One minute...less than a minute and everything was changed.* He had heard that war is hell. Now he knew first hand that it was true.

He heard later that the two boys from Alabama were left sitting there in shock. They had also been blasted with a loud and bloody kind of reality that would color their own views of life forever. Neither had been injured at the time, but a few weeks later, one of them was hurt when his group got too close to a land mine. He ended up in the same hospital compound and came to visit Jean Marc while he was recuperating from his first surgery.

He said, "After you got taken away, we didn't know what to do, so we sat there and waited to see what would happen next. After a little while, two new guys came over and jumped into the hole with us. We introduced ourselves and then settled down for the rest of the night. We talked about it later and figured out that war didn't stop when a player was gone. They sent in more players and it went on like before. The big guns kept up the shelling. The sun came up and us guys opened another box of rations and were glad for the packs of cigarettes and one of the new guys actually liked the ham and eggs in a can."

They both laughed at that because not many guys liked that meal very much.

The doctors told Jean Marc that he would probably carry the physical scars of that night for the rest of his life. He didn't care about the limp so much. He was grateful they didn't cut off his legs. That would have been worse. He couldn't set out traps or hunt too well from one of those rolling chairs. He had already decided that if they took his leg, he was going to carve himself a peg leg like the pirates wore. He wondered how Amy would feel being married to a pirate, or at least somebody who looked like one.

Thinking about it, even now, made the dull ache in his bad leg start to throb. He stretched it out in front of his chair and began to rub it with both hands to relieve the tightness that he still felt every waking moment of every single day.

CHAPTER TEN

The doctors didn't tell him much about dealing with the emotional scars. A man from the Veterans Administration told him that he was eligible for some visits with a psychologist, but Jean Marc was not interested in talking to strangers. He was a private kind of man. That meant that dealing with his emotional issues would be pretty much left up to him to handle on his own. Having never been what he called "a thinker," he wasn't quite sure how or where to begin. He had prayed and thanked God for the doctors who were able to put his body back together. He felt that his mind would heal itself as soon as he got home and held Amy in his arms again. Heal and Go Home became his first parts of "The Plan." It gave him the strength he needed to get through the rest of his time in the hospitals.

Well, now he was home and Amy was married to Pierre Autement and he had to start over. Tomorrow he would get up early and go out to set out the traps and maybe hunt or fish a little and begin his journey to make a new life. He decided that the solution to his problem would be to make a lot of money. That had always helped before. He liked the idea of having a lot of money. Money would help his feelings if nothing else. He would buy his brand new car and drive to Breaux Bridge where Pierre and Amy lived and show her what she had missed. It was a silly and childish thought but it made him smile as he thumped his cigarette butt into the water. He heard the old bull alligator from around the curve toward his parents' house make his evening call again. That old gator had lived there as long as he could remember. He never seemed to bother anyone, he was just always there.

He looked up in the clear dark sky and found the North Star and the Big Dipper and Orion. In the Army he had learned to use the stars for navigation, so now he liked to look at the sky. There was another flash of a shooting star, a silver streak in the dark sky; however, something was odd about it. It seemed too low and was brighter than he remembered and it moved awfully fast. But he dusted off his pants and went inside to bed. He would love to reach the point where he closed his eyes and slept peacefully without seeing the faces of those who died, both friend and foe. Sleep used to come easily. Now it came rarely and was usually interrupted by pain or vivid nightmares. *Tomorrow is the beginning of my new life,* he thought. *It will get better. It has to.*

CHAPTER ELEVEN

The next morning, he got up early, in spite of the fact that he had spent most of the night tossing and turning in his bed. Even with little sleep, he was anxious to get out into the wild swampy places to set his traps. Maybe it was only the excitement of a fresh start but he wanted to make the best of it, whatever it was. The first day or so after his arrival back home had been used up quickly with getting settled and seeing old friends. Getting back to work was both an opportunity to make some money and a chance to see how much the swamp had changed while he was gone. His papa had said one place they used to go to hunt was now completely under water and the trees were dying and he wanted to see that for himself.

After being away for so long, that empty hole in his heart and in his life was screaming to be filled up with something, anything, to make life bearable again. Maybe hard work would renew his spirit. After all he had seen and heard and done over the past few years, he was not even sure that his own brand of normal still existed. But if it did exist, he would find it out there in the swamp. The sooner he got started, the sooner he might get a taste of it.

He sat on a board seat of his homemade pirogue worn smooth by years of Thibodaux bottoms. He used a hickory paddle that had been carved by hand by his own papaw to push out of the little cove that surrounded his home and out into the slow current of the channel. It was hard work and he realized that he was out of practice. Most of his physical therapy had concentrated on getting his legs back to working, and his back and arms were not as strong as they used to be. A few days of paddling his boat would fix that, he thought, and dug the paddle into the brown swirling water and pulled with all his might. When he got tired, he would stop paddling and rest a minute to look around him. The sun was slowly rising over the trees and the morning fog was an eerie mist that floated above both the water and land. The locals called it the devil's breath. It might look a little scary to some, but it was very familiar to him and he liked it. The dappled sunlight and the low-lying fog were beautiful to him. He breathed in the pungent odors of the muddy water and the air above it and watched as a big green bullfrog jumped off a partially submerged log and plopped into the water as he passed by.

He could feel his spirits lifting as he took it all in. The swamp was more than pretty scenery, it was HOME. He leaned his head back and yelled as loud as he could just because he could. "Ahh-Eeeeeee!"

The wildlife went crazy all around him and he could not help laughing out loud, adding more of his own noise to the mix. The birds in the trees screeched and squawked and flew off their perches and the turtles sunning on the floating logs slid into the water. Yelling like that felt so good that he did it again.

"Hey dere, swamp! Dis is me…Jean Marc Thibodaux, and I made it through dat damned ole war and now I'm back! AAAayyyyeeee…" His loud mellow voice tore through the swampy forest the same as it had done a moment before. It was good to be back where he knew that he belonged. He was feeling better already.

CHAPTER TWELVE

"Yo, Thibodaux! Shut up with that racket, boy!"

"Who dat?" Jean Marc yelled back as his head swiveled on his neck. He located the direction of the sound but could not see the caller. He wasn't afraid. The voice was familiar to him, but the sounds were all bouncing from tree to tree and he did not recognize it in the confusion.

"Me dat, you fool...like you ain't heard my voice all your damned life," yelled Boo Landry, his best friend and hunting companion for as long as he could remember.

"You've done scared away every critter worth huntin' in this whole damned swamp! You want my family to go hungry because of your big mouth?"

Boo, grinning, stepped out from behind a big oak tree with his rifle in the crook of his arm. They shook hands and gave each other a manly hug and pat on the back and chatted for a short while and then went in opposite directions. Boo was on a grocery hunt and it was true that Jean Marc's loud outbursts had more than likely emptied out the shelves of this particular store. He headed back up north to find some squirrels or rabbits for supper tonight.

CHAPTER THIRTEEN

As Jean Marc continued going west in his own exploring, he saw a flash of silver through the trees and ran toward it to see what it was, but saw only a shiny blurred image for a fraction of time. He doubted his own eyes. He thought he saw a man in a shiny suit standing very still for a moment, but could not get close enough to get a good look at him. He went crashing through the brush and the mud to try to catch up but did not see anything to tell him which way to go.

He yelled, "Hello... is anybody there?" but no one answered. It wasn't scary, but it was awfully peculiar. Then he figured he must have been imagining it. He had never seen anyone running around in the swamp in a silver suit before. He had never seen anyone wear a silver suit before. It didn't make any sense at all. But the animals were quiet and not even the insects made a sound. That was peculiar too.

He jumped over a little stream and then found one of his old favorite trapping places and began to set out two of his new spring traps. He put one on each side of the water but spread out so they weren't too close together. He saw plenty of good signs. There were raccoon and beaver tracks all around the area. Both kinds of pelts brought good money. His leg hurt a little as he bent and stretched to put the traps down and get them settled and covered with grass, but he expected that. It would take a while for the muscles to get stronger. He was not going to let that stop him from doing his work. He would find a way to overcome that obstacle the same as he had managed to overcome the other problems that came up in his life. The pain brought back memories of that night as it always did, but he worked through it and kept doing his job as the thoughts passed through his mind.

After Jean Marc was injured, the medics took him to a large tent set up as a field hospital, where he got the first basic medical attention. They cleaned him up and stitched the cuts and removed the pieces of metal that had imbedded in his flesh. They tried to set his leg, but the bones were so badly damaged that they had to send him to a larger hospital to have them repaired surgically. Over and over, Jean Marc begged the doctors not to cut off his leg. The surgeon explained that he was going to try to piece the bones together and hold them in place with metal plates and screws. It worked. A couple of weeks after the surgery, they sent him to an even larger hospital where he stayed for several long months of physical therapy. Jean Marc thought it was interesting that they could put his leg back together like it was a piece of machinery, but it didn't matter to him how they did it as long as they found a way. When he pressed his thumb deeply into the damaged muscles of his calf, he thought that he could feel the plate there, hard and foreign. But the metal pieces did the job and he soon began to trust them to hold him together. Having a few metal parts was much better than losing his leg, so he was grateful. Modern medicine was a wonderful thing. They were using sulfa drugs and even penicillin to fight infection and new surgical techniques were saving many arms and legs that would have had to be amputated in previous wars. He had good doctors and with their help, his body had healed. He was grateful. He didn't want to imagine going through the rest of his life unable to walk or run when he chose and he honestly hadn't wanted to look like a pirate.

Even in the hospital, when he finally was able to walk again, he did a lot of it. He had never been one to sit in one place for very long. He had limped up and down the long ward room filled with the beds of other men who were sick or injured. He stopped and chatted with many of them. Most of the patients had no other friends or family living near enough to come visit them. They were from all over the United States and he met a lot of interesting people. They were scared and lonely young men who had injuries, just like him. He would give encouragement to those who were feeling blue and he would pray with those who wanted to pray. He asked for and received paper and envelopes and wrote letters for some and gave them to the nurses to mail to the patients' loved ones. Doing those things kept him busy and made him feel useful. The nurses were grateful for the help and after a time, they let him have the run of the place. Several times he held the hands of those who were dying and prayed for them when they passed on. Those times were the hardest, but he did not want to see any of his hospital companions die alone. There was enough of that on the battlefields. Even in the hospitals, the doctors and nurses were so busy that they often could not spare the time to comfort the dying, when the living needed them more. Jean Marc was so thankful for the fact that he was alive, and that his injuries had been repaired, that he felt obligated to do whatever he could to help.

The Catholic chaplain, Father Emory, asked him once if he had ever considered the priesthood. He hadn't. But there for a few minutes, he did think about it a little. He could understand the attraction of the priesthood for some. Helping others gave deep satisfaction and made him feel like he was helping the cause and that he was giving back a little of the good care that he had received. But he had a life back home and was anxious to get back to it and he was not interested in the priesthood as a permanent way of life. Besides…there was Amy to think about and a life of celibacy did not fit into those plans at all. Father Emory helped him to understand his feelings about the things he had seen and done during his time in battle. He told Jean Marc that God has a special place in his heart for the soldiers. They are sent into battle to do things they had been taught were wrong and then many of them felt guilt afterwards. But God knows what is in a man's true heart. He forgives the deeds that a soldier has to perform. It made Jean Marc feel better to know that. It started the process of his forgiving himself for what he had done and it let him know that God was a loving God who would not punish him for the things he did under orders from his commanding officer. It helped a lot.

CHAPTER FOURTEEN

Finally, after months that seemed like years, Jean Marc was released from the hospital and was sent home. The war was ending and he and many others were being mustered out of the Army. Home—it seemed strange that one little four-letter word could evoke so much emotion in a grown man. After all his experiences, he seemed to care more about people and feelings than he had before he left home. He found himself getting tears in his eyes when things disturbed him. He figured there were some who would say that meant that he was getting soft. The nurses had told him that it was normal after all that he had been through. He could only hope. Not much about his life these past three years had felt normal. It still seemed to him that he may have forgotten what normal feels or sounds like or even smells like. For months after he was in the hospital, he would jump at loud noises. It had taken time to get accustomed to the aromas of Army life from body odor to cordite and death but then he had to teach his nose to accept the hospital smells of disinfectant and bandages and even blood and infection along with other body fluids. Now he was back to the old familiar sounds of the swamp and the aromas of mud and wood smoke and Mama's cooking. He liked those much better.

He was transported back to the States on a crowded troop ship. A lot of the men onboard had been injured like

Jean Marc and so they gathered on the deck as they came into New York Harbor because quite a few of them had not believed that they would ever see home again. When they spotted the statue of Lady Liberty, they all started to cheer. Many had tears in their eyes. Jean Marc was one of them.

That led his mind back to Amy Benoit. He didn't want to think about Amy at all today. There were too many traps to set and too many other things he had to think about to get bogged down in things that he could not change. He pushed Amy out of his mind completely and went on with his work.

After his traps were set, he found one of his old favorite fishing places and spent some time there casting his throwing net. It felt awkward at first but his arm and back muscles were getting stronger and after a few tries, he got the old rhythm back and soon managed to catch enough fish to feed his family supper. He had several ways to catch fish. He liked to use a running line of hooks for the catfish and enjoyed using a handheld line or a pole for the sac-a-lait or for bream. The net caught up everything in its path and was always filled with surprises. Even the prehistoric looking gar with his mouth full of sharp teeth was good eatin' if it was cooked right. Turtle soup was something even more special. He had heard that down in New Orleans, the fancy restaurants sold turtle soup for very high prices. He made a mental promise that one day he was going down there and get a bowl. There was no way that a fancy restaurant could make a better turtle soup than his mama and he wanted to eat some and compare it for himself.

Last night, his mother had reminded him of her offer to

cook the fish if he would catch them. It was an offer that she made often to both her sons from the time they were first old enough to fish. Jean Marc brought home a lot of fish over the years. Aaron didn't bring home as many.

His brother Aaron, who was four years older, was more inclined to spend his time caring for his fighting cocks than to use it for fishing or trapping. Aaron was always looking for an angle or a deal and a way to get out of hard work. His papa used to tell him that he worked harder at getting out of work than it would have taken to do the job in the first place. Jean Marc and Aaron plainly had different ways of looking at many things. It had been that way forever, but they were brothers and cared about each other.

After seeing the real suffering of the people in Europe during the war, Jean Marc had come to the conclusion that his own people were blessed by having been exiled down here in this place of water and mud. Their coming may not have been by choice, but it is a paradise. Before he left home, he had loved it but now after his experiences, he appreciated it more than ever.

Jean Marc meandered slowly through the twisting waterways he had known since childhood. He was having fun exploring. When he was younger, he would leave home early in the morning to spend all of his time out in the swamp with Boo and Elloi. Hunting and fishing were not only entertaining for him and his friends, but they put food on the tables when there was little money to buy food from the stores. They almost never arrived back home without something to show for their day.

This swampland didn't belong to any of them except

in their own minds, but they claimed it as their own territory and each one of them knew every tree and tributary. Many of his friends and family did own the plots of land where they built their small wooden houses but the rest of the swampy place was public land or water. They figured that they had as much right to be here as anyone and they enjoyed that right to the fullest. Many of them lived on floating houseboats and had no real address. They used the land closest to where the houseboat was tied up and stayed until the land played out or until they found someplace they liked better and then they would move on.

The truth was, at least as far as he knew, that nobody wanted anything from the swamp anymore. Unless someone found a need for the smelly black oil that seeped out of the ground and sometimes bubbled up through the water or a use for the acres of second-growth cypress timber that made it worth the effort to brave the alligators and mosquitoes to get it, then the swamp would stay exactly as it had been forever. All the huge cypress trees had been cut down in the 1920s and had left the landscape a mess of stumps and new growth with canals and ditches running everywhere. The canals were dug to provide easier access to the virgin timber. They cut down all the biggest trees. Nearly twenty years had passed since they left and the trees were still trying to fill in the gaps. Some people said it would never be the same again. It was sad to see. There didn't seem to be much left that anyone would want. A few of his friends still made a small amount from pulling the long gray moss from the trees. They collected the moss to be sold for use as stuffing for furniture. But even that was now in short supply. A lot of the moss disappeared with the old timber that had been harvested years before and now it was not easy to find the amounts needed by suppliers. The new foam rubber cushions had become popular and were preferred by some because they were more comfortable, and so another job was being lost in Butte La Rose. Even so, Jean Marc saw no reason to foresee anything changing in his own life. He expected to live out his life time here in this wilderness, just as his parents were doing. Other than the rise and fall of the tides and the occasional hurricane, nothing much happened in the swamp that would be worth writing about in the newspapers. And that was fine with the residents. They preferred it to be that way. It left them to their fishing and hunting.

CHAPTER FIFTEEN

He drifted with the slow current for a while and then turned his boat into the even more sluggish tributary off to the right side and made his way to the big old hollowed-out cypress tree that he had used all his life as a landmark. He was glad to see that it was still there. His approach frightened a great blue heron that lifted his enormous wings and flew away.

The solitary cypress tree stump stood there surrounded by a group of knobby growths from the roots that stuck out of the water like a group of children at its feet. Using a braided rope, he tied his pirogue to one of the taller cypress knees and climbed out to the soggy ground to explore a little.

This land was so blessed that his people never truly went hungry if they were willing to go out and find the food. The winter months were mild and the fish were plentiful as well as the alligators and turtles and shrimp and crabs and crawfish and oysters. There were deer and wild hogs and squirrels and rabbits in addition to ducks and geese and quail. Many of the residents kept flocks of chickens too. There was also the corn and onions and peppers and okra and other vegetables they grew. The residents shared their bounty and the swamp had always been good to them. The houses were built on tall piers over the swampy sections and the high and dry land was used for growing the vegetables or grazing the cattle. Before the war, Jean Marc had made most of his money from trapping the fur-bearing animals and selling the skins during the colder months. During the warmer months, he acted as a guide for tourists and fishermen. During the fall, he led hunting parties. He did pretty well before the war and expected that he would make enough for his needs now that he was home.

He took the fish home and he and his father cleaned them and got them ready for his mama to cook. There was enough fish that when Aaron and his family came by for a visit on their way back from Lafayette, Mama invited them to stay for dinner. She dredged the fish in corn meal and fried them up all crispy and brown. The sliced tomatoes from the garden and red beans cooked with sausage and ladled over fluffy white rice were flavors that Jean Marc had missed during his time away. He ate his share and probably a little more. There was a lot of dinnertime conversation and the children sat there quietly, watching the faces of everyone else at the table. Aaron's wife, Patrice, cut up little bites of fish and put one bean at a time on the table, so the two-and-a-half-year-old baby girl could pick it up with her own fingers and put it into her own mouth.

Mama said, "Jean Marc, I was wondering if you got to eat any real French cooking while you were in France."

He laughed a little.

"Mama, I didn't get many chances to eat fancy food. Most of my food came from a chow line if I was lucky and from little green ration cans if I wasn't. But there was one day that I asked for some time off. I explained to my commanding officer that this was our family's old home town and asked for permission to go try and find my relatives and he let me go. We were there waiting for some other units to join us and there wasn't much to do until they arrived. I asked everybody I saw on the street until I finally found a family who claimed to be our relatives, but honestly Mama, they had the right names, but they didn't sound or look like anyone I would have ever recognized. But then, we have to understand those people were having a hard time. There was a war going on where they were, yeah. They had to live with guns going off and bombs dropping all around them. They were curious about us too but didn't seem to understand much about where we live or how different it is. France is nothing like this place. The only places they know about in the States are New York and Hollywood. They don't know about Louisiana at all. Another thing is... they talk funny."

The room filled with laughter at that.

Aaron said, "A few years back, I met some tourists from France and had the same problem. They talk too fast and they use different words for things. They don't eat no crawfish or *boudin* either."

They all had another laugh. The two little girls clapped their hands together and squealed, "We like cwaw-fish, Daddy. We like *boudin,* Daddy," and everyone joined in.

Jean Marc said, "I understood most of what they said, but I had to ask them to explain a lot of things. We may speak French, but it is sure not the same French that they speak over there. I ate dinner with them one Sunday after going to Mass but the food was not anything like your cooking, Mama. The meal was OK but there wasn't much meat and it was not seasoned very much. But again, you gotta remember, that was wartime and they were struggling to find food at all. I got a chicken wing and didn't ask for second helpings. I just made sure that I got back in time for chow time. They had eaten up most of their livestock and even a fat chicken was hard to find. Mama, they can't go out back in the woods over there and shoot something for supper. We got it good here, yeah.

"Oh! And another thing, Aaron, now I understand a little more about why you got so upset about me joining the Army. In Europe, the governments took over everything. I see now that you were afraid that if the Government here got wise to us Cajuns being here and not so many registered with the draft, they might have come after everybody and made them get registered. You said it would be exactly like the other times when the Government dragged our people out of their homes and sent them off to fight in their wars. Seeing how those people over there were living so poor made me real thankful that we ended up here, no matter how it happened. The Lord has been good to our people, yeah. We got everything we need right here around us. We're doing a lot better than those who were left behind over there. I am glad that we ended up down here in this ole swamp."

The table got quiet for a few seconds as everyone thought about that.

CHAPTER SIXTEEN

Jean Marc realized that he had caused the quiet and said, "Papa, I got my traps put out. I am going to go check them in the morning and I am hoping to get some skins to sell to Ole Man Breaux like I used to. Is he still buying furs?"

"Yeah, son, he is and he passed by here and was asking me the other day if you were gonna be trapping this year. I told him, yeah. He says you will have less competition than you used to have, 'cause a lot of the old guys quit trapping and the younger ones don't seem to be interested in it much. He says the prices are up too. You might do OK with that. For sure, nobody else is doing good with fishing. The salt water is coming into the canals and messing things up real bad. You can catch enough to have a meal but it is hard to catch enough to sell to the big buyers that want it for the restaurants and stuff. The fish that don't like salt water are all moving back up the river. The fancy restaurants are not interested in gar and catfish. Me, I like a good catfish."

Jean Marc said, "That's good about the furs. I'm glad to hear it. I want to save up enough money to buy me a car."

His mama's face lit up and she asked, "A car? What on earth do you want a car for, *Sha?*"

He got up from the table and took his mama in his arms and swung her around like they were dancing. The two little girls squealed and laughed while clapping their hands together the way they always did when they got excited, because they thought it was funny seeing Jean Marc swing his mama around like that.

"I want me a car, so I can take my mama for a ride in a shiny new auto-mo-bile instead of a truck. I want me a car, so I can drive my mama and papa to Baton Rouge and take us all to see a picture show."

His papa snorted and said, "Wasn't it just a minute ago you said that we got everything we need right in our own backyard? I don't need to go to Baton Rouge. There ain't nothing over there I need."

His mama laughed and said, "Well, then, you can stay home, Jacque Thibodaux. I want to go to see me a picture show. Sophie LeBlanc said she saw one of them moving pictures with that movie star, Clark Gable, in it. She said he is one handsome man. Yep, I want to go see Clark Gable in a picture show, Jean Marc."

Jean Marc laughed and said, "Then that is what we will do. We will go see that handsome man, Clark Gable in a movie show."

Papa said, "I don't believe that you would think he was so handsome if you saw him in real live person. I hear them movie star men wear that make-up on their faces, just like the women."

Mama said, "You are telling a lie, Jacque Thibodaux. They don't neither wear no make-up. That is just plain crazy and I don't believe it."

They had fun arguing back and forth as they sopped up some good ole cane syrup with a hot buttered biscuit and called it dessert and finished it off with a cup of chicory-laced coffee with lots of cream from their own cow's milk.

After dinner Papa asked to be excused.

He said, "I need to go find that handsome Clark Gable and borrow his lipstick. I left mine outside in the truck."

They all laughed so hard that they banged on the table and got tears in their eyes. A natural comedian, Papa was always telling a tale. He could sing and play the fiddle too. Papa Jacque was good at a lot of things, but then Cajun men were normally pretty self-reliant. They had a natural sense of how things worked and could generally fix any-thing or make anything they needed. They had to be that way to survive. If they could not figure out how to make what they needed, they generally did without it.

After dinner, they all found their usual places on the living-room furniture or on the floor and listened to the big round-shouldered console radio for a while. *The Louisiana Hay Ride Show* was good entertainment for the whole family. Even Aaron and Patrice's two children quietly sat or lay on a blanket on the floor by their parents' chairs and lis-tened to the music and laughed when everyone else laughed at the comedy routines until they finally gave up and fell asleep right where they lay.

Jean Marc said his goodbyes and accepted the brown paper bag of leftovers that his mama had saved for him. He made his way back to his own little place to sleep. He couldn't help but think a little about Amy and try to imagine what their family life would have been like. He wondered if they would have had children. He tried to pic-ture them all gathered around the radio in their own house like they had been tonight. It used to be so easy to imagine scenes like that, but now it didn't seem to look right in his mind anymore. He wanted a family. He wanted that kind of lifestyle. Mama said there would be someone for him, and he sure hoped she was right. He wished that whoever the girl out there waiting for him was, she'd hurry up and find him. He was lonesome and tired of feeling that way.

CHAPTER
SEVENTEEN

The next morning he grabbed a piece of bread and some leftover fish and a cup of fresh drip coffee for breakfast and then left to check the traps he had set the day before. Paddling his boat, he followed the same route as yesterday but today he was feeling a little better about the future. He had enjoyed the dinner with his parents and his brother's family the night before, and some of the strangeness of having been away was slowly wearing off.

As he rounded a curve in the river, a cloud of white herons lifted into the air all at once and he could not help but grin from ear to ear. The sheer beauty of it was almost like going to church. He said an "Our Father" and made the sign of the cross and felt completely at home. He paddled when the water was deep and stood up to push a long pole into the shallow bottom to push his flat-bottomed boat through the water when he had to, and meandered again from place to place collecting his harvest of raccoons, beavers and even a couple of nutria, the animals recently imported from South America. Some of them had escaped from their cages at the fur farms and were living in the swamp. They had thick fur a lot like the beaver and were said to be bringing in good prices. He reset each of the traps, but more quickly than yesterday. He had to get the dead animals home so that he could get them skinned and scraped and then the hides were salted down to stop the deterioration. Not every trap had caught something but there were enough that he was pleased. It felt good to be working toward a goal again.

After going over things in his mind last night while trying to will himself to sleep, he had even forgiven Amy for marrying his friend, Pierre Autement, instead of waiting for him. He tried to believe that it didn't matter to him anymore. He thought if he could get the chance to ask her why it had happened, he would be able to lay the whole thing to rest. But he wasn't going out of his way to see her. That would have looked like he cared too much and he would not give Amy nor Pierre the satisfaction of knowing how much he cared. It would get better...one day. He did understand how it had happened. He had brought it all on himself by asking Pierre Autement to watch out for his girl while he was away. Even so, he wanted to hear her say the words. He wanted to see the guilt in her eyes when she tried to explain. It felt like the whole thing hurt his pride more than his heart. It was a disappointment but now he was not even sure that what he had felt was love at all. There was a nagging fear inside him that he wished would go away, but he didn't know how to make it happen.

His mama had said that it only meant that there is someone special out there waiting for him.

Jean Marc hoped that his mama was right.

He didn't share his fearful feelings with anyone. Just because a man understands a thing that brings him pain does not mean that the pain goes away. If Amy felt that he was not worth waiting for then, could that mean that no woman would ever be able to love him forever? Jean Marc did not believe in divorce. He wanted the kind of love that stands the test of time like his own parents had. Wasn't that what everyone wanted?

CHAPTER EIGHTEEN

While he was resetting a trap, he caught a flash of shining light in his peripheral vision. He watched as the flash of light went from the sky down toward the ground. It was the same kind of flash that he had seen before. But wishing stars don't usually show up in the daytime, he thought. He heard a loud crashing noise in the woods and felt the ground quaking beneath his boots. He got the trap settled in at the marshy water's edge and headed off toward the sound. After a short hike, he saw the glint of metal shining through the trees. His curiosity got the better of him and he carefully high-stepped over and through the tangle of undergrowth and waded through water and mud to reach the place where he had seen the flash of silver.

He stood on the edge looking down into a very wide but shallow hole in the earth. There was a large metal object half buried there in the muddy crater. It was shiny polished silver and had strange writing etched into the metal. It didn't resemble any aircraft that he had ever seen, but he seemed to know instinctively that this was a flying machine of some kind that had crash landed. His first instinct was to look for survivors. He climbed over the vines and touched the metal. He banged on it with his fist, expecting to hear it sound like a hollow oil drum. It sounded more solid than he had expected. He laid his hand flat on the widest part. The metal on top was warm but not nearly as hot as he had expected. He sensed that someone was watching him. He looked around and shouted a loud, "Hello-oo... is anybody in there? Are you all right? Do you need help?" He got no answer. In fact, he suddenly realized that the swamp was totally quiet. That was an extremely rare situation. There was nothing making noise, no droning insects, no birds, no sound of any kind. He felt odd, like somebody was watching him. The hairs on the back of his neck stood up and he carefully picked his way back to his boat and left as quickly as possible. He finished making his rounds and got his skinning and other chores done as fast as he could, but he thought about the shiny metal air machine all day until he fell asleep that night.

His original thought was to talk to his father and brother about going back with him the next day to pull the mysterious aircraft out of the mud. While he was working on his hides, he decided to keep his find to himself. He wasn't sure of his reason for keeping quiet, but decided to go back alone to see what he could figure out before telling anyone about what he had seen. Some would have called it a "gut-feeling."

The next morning as usual, he was up with the sun. He drank his coffee and ate a SPAM sandwich before going out.

SPAM, a chopped ham loaf in a can, was one of the new "store-bought" foods that he had learned to like while in the Army. It didn't need refrigeration and was cheap to buy and he had developed quite a taste for the stuff when he ate it in his K-rations in the field.

He packed up his Army entrenching tool, a short folding

shovel…and a roll of strong chain as well as a special tool he used for stretching fence wire that he called a "come-along." He wanted to wrap a chain around some part of the machine and wrap more chain around a tree and pull that thing out of the mud by himself. He bypassed his traps this time and headed straight to the area where he found the downed aircraft. He tied up the pirogue and sloshed and high-stepped to the spot as fast as he could and was disappointed that there was nothing to see. The crater was there with a deep puddle of brown water in the center of the depression, but the large silver thing that he believed to be some kind of aircraft was gone. He poked through the mud and walked around the edge but saw nothing unusual.

That made him VERY glad that he had not spoken to his father and brother about this find. It would have been hard to explain in the first place, but even worse if they had all come here to see a real spaceship and found nothing. He would have looked foolish and felt even more so.

Aaron would be saying that he had come home shell-shocked. That was the name they gave to those who were severely affected mentally or emotionally by what they had done or seen during the war. He had met some of those lost souls in the hospitals while he was recuperating from his own physical problems. There were lots of soldiers sitting in veterans hospitals all over the country who could no longer function in the real world. They were pitiful hollow shells of men. It was like they had been totally overwhelmed by their experiences. After seeing them, he had immediately decided that he would rather have come home in a coffin than to come home shell-shocked.

He looked around the areas nearby and saw nothing there either except the usual flora and fauna. A big nutria-rat sat up to look at him with his beady brown eyes. He held onto a root of some kind with his little front paws. Jean Marc told him to go a little over to the left and there would be a nice surprise waiting for him. The animal looked at him and opened his mouth to yawn, showing his enormous orange teeth. He was not interested in finding the traps this morning or becoming a collar on some lady's new coat. Jean Marc laughed and told him to go home to his rat family and to stay out of trouble. The animal waddled off toward a big uprooted tree and Jean Marc laughed out loud. He listened for anything unusual and noticed that the sounds of the swamp were in full chorus this morning. He heard the droning whine of the insects and the birds and even the frogs were singing today. Whatever the thing in the hole had been, it was gone now. So he went back to check his traps and then shot several of the big brown and gray squirrels for supper and headed back the way he had come.

As he made the last turn to get back into the main channel, he felt the hair on the back of his neck stand up again. He also noticed the peculiar silence. He didn't see anything moving except a water snake zigzagging toward the riverbank, but he felt a presence and it seemed strange and unnatural. He looked in a circle around him and peered deep into the growth of trees and bushes but saw nothing unusual and continued on to his parents' place. Something odd was definitely going on around the swamp.

He was still not ready to discuss it with anyone. There

had been a time when he would have told his parents anything. Maybe he was out of the habit or maybe war had a way of changing the way a man thinks. It changed the way a man reacted to those thoughts too.

CHAPTER NINETEEN

While standing on the bottom step of his parents' house, Jean Marc called out, "Mama, I got you some squirrels."

He heard her quick short steps across the cypress boards of the floor of the front room and onto the porch to the steps where he stood.

"Awww, *Sha*, *merci*, my baby, thank you, those are nice fat ones, yeah. They would make a good stew. Come on in the house and have some supper with us."

"No, mama, I have skins to work on and I am too dirty. I would mess up your floor. I know you just swept it, 'cause you do it 'bout this time every day," he chuckled. His mama was a stickler for keeping to a routine. She had always said that it was a good way to make sure all the chores got done.

His dog had been staying with his parents while he was gone and he called out to him now, "Come on, Chili, it's time you got your scrawny butt back home, where you belong. Sooner or later you'll have to get used to my cookin' again."

Chili happily scrambled into the pirogue, making it rock back and forth, and then finally took his usual place stretched out in the bottom.

His mama looked at him with a spark of humor in her eyes and yelled to the dog, "Chili, don't you worry, *Sha*, if you get hungry you can still come back home to eat." She laughed to herself and headed back towards the kitchen with the squirrels. If Papa was around, he would clean them and dress them for cooking but if not, then Mama was as skilled and as willing to do the job herself. Living so close to nature made a person, even a small and delicate lady like his mama, learn skills that they might not ever need in a city. His mother could do her part in dressing a deer or butchering a hog on Saturday and sit in her usual place in church on Sunday looking like a lady who never dirtied her little hands.

Jean Marc and his dog headed on out into the channel and back up to their own little piece of paradise. Chili would let him know if anything or anyone unusual was around the cabin, but he was also good company, and Jean Marc was still finding himself more than a little bit lonesome since his return.

His old hunting dog was known all over the parish for his nose. Tomorrow he was taking Chili with him to check things out around that big hole in the ground. If there was something out there, Chili would find it.

But first, Jean Marc needed to find a way to settle his mind and get some sleep.

He opened the leather-bound trunk at the foot of his bed and found the black case that had been there since before his papaw passed away. He carefully unclipped the bow from its place in the case and ran his rough fingers over the wood of the violin with reverence and love. Papaw had started teaching him to play before he was old enough for his fingers to reach the strings to make the chords. It was a sweet but painful thing to draw the bow across the strings and make that first note that night. His heart was sad but it was satisfying in another way. Papaw had given him the gift of music and no one could take that away. He played a few sad songs and let the tears flow unchecked. Lately he had been having a hard time with his emotions. It was not something he was accustomed to but playing the old songs helped somehow. He could almost see his papaw tapping his finger on the arm of the old rocking chair and raising one heel to the rhythm of the music as he played. It helped him to feel more grounded and less uncertain. It made him feel stronger and even more glad and grateful to be home. When he felt ready, he carefully packed the instrument away in the trunk and crawled between his blankets to sleep.

CHAPTER TWENTY

After his morning meal, Jean Marc packed a canvas tote-bag with his folding shovel and other gear, like he had done the day before. Chili jumped aboard and settled in his usual place. Chili knew the routine; he had ridden in pirogues since he was a pup and would sit very still. The plan was to take Chili to the spot where the crater was, to allow the dog to sniff around and get the smell in his nose. Then he wanted Chili to seek out that odor again and see if he could find anything else that smelled like that. It was no different from sniffing out a possum or a raccoon. Jean Marc had confidence that Chili would be able to find whatever it was that crashed that silver aircraft into the swampy mud. What he would do if they did find something or someone was a whole 'nother problem. He would have to deal with that if it happened, but he brought his rifle and would keep it handy just in case.

It was a warm and pleasant October day with a hint of rain in the air. Chili looked around as they followed the water farther back into the swamp. He soon settled down on his belly to snooze. When they rounded the curve that led to the crater, Chili woke up suddenly and whined. He looked at Jean Marc and whined again and put his head down on his outstretched paws.

Jean Marc asked him, "Whatza matter, boy? What you

hear? You see something scaredy out there? We need to go find it."

A serious hunting dog, Chili was usually not afraid of anything. He grew up with guns going off all around him. He was familiar with the smell of blood from every kind of animal that they hunted and had even fought with a big ole raccoon when he was younger and never gave an inch. That coon would have probably killed him if Jean Marc's father hadn't shot it. He gave his son a well-deserved lecture on protecting his dog too. It was disturbing to see this same animal whining in the bottom of the boat. He tied up the pirogue and encouraged Chili to come with him to the crater site by clapping his hands together and trying to sound eager.

"Come on, boy, let's go see what we can find in there." Chili followed but he was not in a hurry and not at all happy about it. He sniffed and then snorted as though he didn't like the smell. Jean Marc breathed in deeply to see if he recognized any kind of unusual odor, but didn't smell anything except the usual aromas of rotten eggs from the decaying vegetation in the mud and cypress woods and water with a slightly fishy aftertaste that stayed in his nose.

Jean Marc jumped down into the crater and called to his dog. Chili ran around whining and stood at the outside edge of the hole and dug with his paws and barked nervously and then looked at Jean Marc as if he was supposed to do something, but Jean Marc could not figure out what the dog wanted him to do...except leave the area. A misty rain had begun to fall and the hole was beginning to slowly fill with water from the drainage. Before long, it would be just another mud-hole in the swamp.

He walked around sloppily down inside the slippery depression and looked more closely at the mud and plant material. He began digging to see what he could find. There was a burned mud crust around the back of the crater that was baked as hard as a piece of pottery. Something had gotten very hot inside this hole. He looked closely at the charred wood and burned leaves from the area. It reminded him of the effect of a flamethrower like he had seen in the Army. Chili was watching his every move. He held a piece of the charred wood up to let the dog sniff it but Chili snorted at it and turned his head away strangely and whined and put his head down on his paws again. He didn't want anything to do with the strange odors from the muddy depression.

It was disappointing but after another few shovels full of dirt brought nothing up but mud and the usual earthworms, snails and debris from the trees and vines, there didn't seem to be much reason to stay there, so he packed up his shovel and got back into the boat and started toward home. He talked to his dog as he pushed the pole into the mud to give his boat a shove back out into the water. Chili just looked at him with a look on his doggy face that clearly said, "Git us out of here." And they say that a dog can't talk.

So Jean Marc told him, "It's OK, boy, we are going now," and the dog lay down in his regular place again.

As they made the last curve before heading back into the main channel, Chili lifted his head and barked. Jean Marc looked in the same direction as Chili and saw a streak of silver shoot upward across the sky at a very fast rate of speed. He had never seen anything that could move that fast; not even the beautiful airplanes he saw during the war could move that fast. The other peculiar thing was that there was no sound. All of the aircraft he had ever seen had loud engines. The sound from regular airplanes was so loud that it hurt your ears. If that was an aircraft of some kind, it was very quiet. He wondered about what kind of engine could move that fast and not make any sound at all. What kind of fuel would it use? Once again, he was glad that he had not told his friends and family about seeing the large half-buried aircraft, or whatever it was, in the swamp. He would have felt plain stupid if they had gotten there and found nothing. At the same time, the more he thought about it, the more he knew that something very strange was going on. There were too many things that didn't make sense to a common man like himself. Maybe he truly was shell-shocked and just didn't realize it or maybe he was seeing things that didn't exist...or...maybe he was losing his mind. There were half-formed thoughts of spacecraft and little green men and jokes about Martians, but nothing that his mind could accept or even believe.

He asked himself out loud, "That Martian stuff was all a joke...right? Wasn't it a joke? I mean, nobody actually thinks that there's men from outer space that come down here to visit us, do they? Could people be living out there on some other planet? Could they be coming here in small silver airplanes like the one he saw? Why would they do that? What could they want here? Could we all be in danger from these strangers? Or am I imagining all of it?"

CHAPTER TWENTY-ONE

Jean Marc didn't know the answers to any of those questions, but he wasn't about to bring up the topic for discussion with anybody that he knew in Butte La Rose. He looked up into the sky and tried to imagine that other beings were living there in the same way that regular folks were living here on this planet. It was interesting but not something that he was ready or willing to accept as a reality. It did give his mind something to ponder though. Could it be possible?

His papa had always said his own head was full of stories and wild ideas. He said it like he thought that there was something wrong with having a mind that was full of stories and wild ideas, but Jean Marc saw it as being something natural. He had a very active imagination too and that sometimes helped him figure things out. It helped him solve a lot of problems that came up in daily life. It saved his butt a time or two during wartime. That surely could not be thought of as something bad. Could it? The more he thought about it, the more he decided that the strange things going on around him were real. They had to be. These things were not simply a part of his imagination. He saw them. He touched that piece of equipment. He might not talk about it but he was not going to stop looking for clues. Something was going on in the swamp and he was going to get to the bottom of it. He had to know the truth, one way or another.

After he got home, he and Chili went inside and settled down for the night. He thought about going to see his parents, but it didn't seem right to go there every night. Jean Marc was still lonesome. It was worse in the evenings. In the daytime, there was work to do. Work kept a person's body and brain busy and focused, but in the quiet of the evening, the mind wandered and ventured onto topics best not thought of too often.

After a simple supper, he settled down to listen to his own table-top radio for a while. He took himself a dose of Hadacol, a patent medicine that was known for curing what ails you. It tasted terrible, but the man in the Hadacol commercial on the radio said that the taste was part of the cure. Anything that tasted that bad had to be good for you. He didn't like the bitter herbal taste, but he liked the buzz that he got from sipping it. A tablespoon or so of Hadacol made him feel almost the same as when he used to have a few beers. It helped him sleep and right now that meant a lot.

The violin theme song began to play announcing the *Jack Benny Show* was about to start. He liked to hear Mr. Benny and his butler, Rochester, banter back and forth. He wondered how rich a man had to be to have someone work for him at his house all the time. A person would have to be pretty rich to do that, he bet to himself. His hidden coffee can would not hold enough to be that rich. But then he might have to get over his fear of letting the money out of his own possession and put it into a bank. The thought was scary, but a man had to be safe and it was not safe to keep such large amounts of cash on hand that it gave bad people ideas. Fortunately, he did not know any bad people, but still you never know what could make a person take to stealing.

After climbing into his bed, Jean Marc lay there, staring at the plywood ceiling and letting his thoughts continue to ramble around inside his head. The traps were working well for him and he was adding the skins to his collection that was stretched on frames and drying on the outside walls of the cabin and the storage shed. If the warm weather held out for a few more days then he would be ready to take this lot into town and sell them. It would be the first real money he had made since his return.

Before he left for the war, he had made a pretty good living from his hides. Unfortunately, most all of his money had been spent on gifts for Amy and for beer. A few times, he had even wasted large amounts betting on Aaron's fighting roosters. Money had always seemed to be a renewable resource and he didn't worry about it too much. He made the dollars and spent them and then went out and made some more. He owed nothing to anyone and lived mostly for himself. During the time he was away, he had thought about the future and decided that once he and Amy were married things would have to be different. Even though he wasn't getting married right away, he wasn't going to squander away his money like before.

If he ever got rich, he would put the money in the bank, but for the time being, he would be happy to see his coffee can fill up, he thought before his eyes closed and he sank under the waves of sleep.

CHAPTER TWENTY-TWO

The next morning Jean Marc woke up feeling groggy and stumbled to the door to let Chili outside to run. He was a little concerned about the thumping headache he had. Maybe he took a bit more of the Hadacol than was necessary to cure whatever it was that was ailing him last night. He had never been one to have a problem with drinking too much and he felt a little ashamed. He hoped that a good strong cup of coffee would cure the headache. He was spooning the chicory-laced coffee into his tall, white-enameled, drip coffee pot when the dog literally came blasting through the closed back door looking terrified. Chili ran around in circles and whined pitifully. Jean Marc was not at all happy about the door frame being destroyed. He mentally added it to his long list of repairs that the old house needed. Sitting empty during the time that he was away had not done the old place much good. There usually wasn't much of a requirement for a locked door here, anyway, but it was nice to be able to close a door when a cool spell came along. He would repair it eventually. He was more concerned about the strange behavior of his dog... maybe he and his dog were both going crazy. He poured the hot water into the top of his coffee pot to drip through the grounds and took Chili's head in both his hands to see if he was all right. The dog appeared to be OK. But he pulled back from his owner's hands and continued with his whining and running in circles in the middle of the kitchen floor. Jean Marc picked up the broken door frame pieces off the bare wood cypress floor. He walked onto the small back porch to throw the wood pieces out the open doorway and into the backyard.

There was a person, or some kind of being, in a shiny, one-piece suit standing there some thirty feet away. It was hard to call him a man, though he was man-shaped. He wasn't as tall as a regular man, maybe about four feet tall. He had big dark eyes, much bigger than any eyes Jean Marc had ever seen on a man before. He was standing there at the edge of the clearing behind the cabin. He didn't move and he didn't speak. But Jean Marc somehow understood immediately that this being/man-thing had something to do with that silvery aircraft that he had found a few days ago. He was torn between reaching for his shotgun and going out to say hello. It was a very exciting but unsettling experience.

The two of them stood looking at each other for another minute and then suddenly the shiny man-thing was gone. He didn't walk exactly, nor did he fly, but he glided somehow back into darkness of the tree line until he couldn't be seen anymore. Chili whined and turned his head first one way and then another and looked up at his master with a puzzled look on his face.

Still trying hard to wrap his own mind around the whole idea, Jean Marc gave a loud sigh and turned back inside and poured his coffee. He shook his head from side to side, refusing to allow himself to admit what he had seen.

He was more confused and yet he was also more curious about whatever it was that he saw out there. Some people saw pink elephants when they have had too much to drink; maybe he was seeing a little man in a silver suit. He definitely needed to lay off the Hadacol. Perhaps he should play the fiddle a little more and drink a lot less.

CHAPTER
TWENTY-THREE

When in doubt about what to do, you start with the work in front of you. That was another saying that his mother used in times of difficulty. His parents' sayings had guided him through most of his life, so far. There was plenty of work to be done around here, so he was sure to stay busy. Jean Marc was not one to sit still anyway. He never had been. His hands and his mind were never at rest for long. There was always something new to see or do after his chores were done, so he would finish his work as quickly as possible to be free to do whatever else he could find to get into. He still found time to read when he could get his hands on a book and he played the fiddle for his own amusement. He wanted to practice a bit more before playing in public again. He was not quite up to joining in with his friends yet, but it was coming. Music was a big part of his life and he would get back to being a part of that before too much longer. Playing Papaw's fiddle was satisfying. He needed that satisfaction right now.

He finished eating breakfast and then went out to check his traps. That had to take top priority. Do the work in front of you, he thought again. Chili elected to stay in the yard. After facing the enemies in battle, Jean Marc was not about to let one strange-looking little man in a shiny suit keep him from his traps. In fact, a secret part of his mind hoped that he would see the silver man again. He was very curious about him and wanted to find out more.

He spent his time doing his chores but his mind was occupied with dozens of questions about the strange happenings of the past few days. He still had not spoken to anyone about the things he had seen nor had he heard any talk about strange sights or unusual aircraft or peculiar-looking little men in silver suits running around in the swamp either. If anyone else had seen the things he had seen, it stood to reason that he would have heard about it by now. He had learned not to overreact to surprises and to keep his thoughts to himself during his time in the Army. His sergeant used to tell the troops that it was hard to learn anything with your mouth open, but open ears could hear a lot. So he had learned the value of listening. But people talk. Usually they do anyway. Nobody was talking about this and that was even more of a puzzle.

"Am I the only one seeing these things? Why me?" he wondered aloud to himself.

CHAPTER TWENTY-FOUR

After his chores were finished, Jean Marc went to town to hear what he could hear. He paid a visit to the General Store to buy a box of nails to fix the door frame and saw some of the townsfolk that he had not already seen since his return.

"Hey there, Jean Marc, how you been doin', boy? We are glad to see you back home, walkin' on two legs and not in no pine box, that's for sure," said Mr. Begnaud as he slapped Jean Marc on the back and pumped his hand in an eager handshake.

He replied, "Mr. Begnaud, I am very glad to be home walkin' on two legs and not in a pine box, myself. There were a few times that even I was scared that I would never make it home again."

Mr. Begnaud patted him on the back again and nodded his head. He did not let on that there had been times when he also seriously wondered if this young man would come home safely. He and all the other town folks had been worried for Jean Marc. He was the only local boy who had gone to fight. Most of the others did not understand his leaving home to fight in a war that they felt was none of their business. FDR had said that he would keep us out of that war, but in the end, we got into it anyway.

The store owner, Tom Landry, was his best friend Boo's father. He and Boo had always been friends and were always getting into some kind of trouble as kids. Now that they were grown, Tom could truthfully say that both his son, Boo, and his friend, Jean Marc, had grown up to be fine men.

Jean Marc had earned several medals in the war, including the Purple Heart for being injured during that battle in France. He kept them in a box that was stashed in his trunk at the foot of his bed. He had never shown them to a soul. The only real hero that he knew was Eric and he was dead. Jean Marc was a very private man and not at all inclined to brag or even to talk about things like that. If he began to talk, then it could lead to questions and that would make him remember too many things that were best not discussed.

There was not even a hint of any strangeness going on at the store, as far as Jean Marc could tell, but then most of the friends and neighbors simply wanted to tell him they were glad that he was home and safe. That kindness made him feel pretty good. The fact was that if any of them had seen the silver man or even noticed his airplane or airship or whatever it was, no one was talking about it. That most likely meant that no one else had seen it. This small place could be quiet to the point of boredom and anything as unusual as the things he had seen would have set the tongues wagging for sure. A bit of gossip, even if it was not especially juicy, flew through this place faster than a brush fire.

He stopped by his parents' house and stayed for squirrel

stew and rice. Papa was in rare form. Jean Marc was sucking the tender braised meat off a tiny squirrel leg bone when his papa asked in a quiet voice, "You starved that pore dog to death yet?"

Jean Marc said, "No, you know he keeps comin' over here to eat Mama's cookin'. He says he don't like my cookin' no more."

Papa said, "Well, I don't doubt that. I haven't seen you cook anything since you got back home except maybe an egg...looks to me like somebody else likes Mama's cookin' too." He slapped the flat of his hand on the tabletop and laughed out loud.

Mama, said, "Jacque, you leave that boy alone. I am glad to have him at my table and he can sit there every night if he wants to. Besides, he is the one that shot that squirrel you are chewing on."

Papa grinned, put his hands on the edge of the table, leaned back in his chair and said, "Yeah...he did and I am kind of glad to see him sitting in that chair myself."

After dinner Jean Marc sat on the porch for a short time talking with his family and then paddled his way back to his own cabin in the dark. He took his Hadacol and crawled in his bed to sleep. He didn't know what ailed him, but the terrible-tasting medicine seemed to be helping his sleep and that was useful. The truth was that if he went over to his cousin's house and bought himself a bottle of real liquor, he was afraid that he might drink a lot more of it than he should. His spirits were low and he was better off taking the vile-tasting Hadacol than he would have been with a jug of better-tasting homemade whiskey. He needed to get himself straightened out here and not use any of the "medicine" that might be available. Deep inside, he knew that alcohol would not help. Even he knew that it was time he got over the bad times and got on with his life.

CHAPTER
TWENTY-FIVE

The next day was his favorite cousin Marguerite Thibodaux's wedding day. She was marrying her lifelong friend, Paul Landry, who was also related to Jean Marc's best friend, Boo. In the small community of Butte La Rose, Louisiana, it seemed that almost everyone was related to each other either by blood or marriage. Most of the rest of them had grown up together and were almost as close as family. Marguerite had made Jean Marc promise to be there to see them take their vows and he was looking forward to it. When they were younger, she was the little girl cousin that followed him around and got in his way and begged for his attention from the time she was walking. He cared about her and wanted her to be happy. It would also feel good to be in his own church again. There would be a big party after the ceremony and he fully intended to party the night away. Jean Marc bathed and dressed in his best clothes for the wedding and arrived early, in case there was some way he could help out. In this small town a wedding was a very special thing and everyone did his part to make it as memorable as they could.

He even had a pretty porcelain music box to give to Marguerite as a gift. He had bought it in France to give to

Amy. He knew that Marguerite would love the music box. It was the kind of thing that any girl would like.

Father Zachary, who was to perform the ceremony, had known both the bride and the groom and most everyone else in the small village for all of their lives. In fact, in the last thirty-five years or more he had performed all the important ceremonies for a good many of the people who would attend this wedding today, from the christenings to first communions and then their weddings and on to last rites and funerals. He was very pleased to join these two young people in marriage and also looking forward to joining the party for a while afterwards. He would perform a simple traditional Catholic ceremony and try to make it a good one, because the parents of both youngsters always listened carefully and would give him plenty of trouble if they had problems later on. Divorces were almost unheard of in Acadian marriages but if the couples fought a lot they would blame it on the priest and say he did not tie the knot tight enough. This one was going to be tied as tight as he could tie it. He wasn't worried because these two had known each other all their lives and were so much in love that each of them glowed when the other was around.

After the ceremony inside the little white church, the women brought out the food and the men brought out the drinks. There was homemade scuppernong wine and even a few jugs of homemade corn whiskey for all to share. They tried to hide the liquor from the ladies, but the ladies knew it was there. It was a silly game of pretending that had gone on at all the community gatherings for years. The food was put out on the tables that were made up out of lumber stretched across wooden sawhorses and covered with sheets before the ceremony. There was also a big pot of boiling water, seasoned with salt and hot red peppers, ready to receive baskets full of corn on the cob and heads of garlic and potatoes to cook with shrimp and big fat blue crabs. Jean Marc had not sat down to a newspaper-covered table piled high with boiled shrimp and crabs in a long time. He could hardly wait for them to begin cooking. There was also a huge black pot of chicken and sausage gumbo and mounds of fluffy white rice as well as freshly baked bread and a lot of other tasty things like cakes and fried pies. The platters of food were arranged and everyone oooh-ed and ahh-ed over the dishes that each lady brought to every gathering. Each family had a dish that made them famous.

There was one big wedding cake that had a bean baked in it and whoever got the bean in his piece was supposed to be the next to marry. Many times the one who got the bean was already married or was a small child and that made it more fun for all.

The religious ceremony itself was solemn but very well done. Marguerite's parents were proud. The young couple was nervous but happy. The knot was tied as tight as a knot could be. Everyone in the village offered them blessings and teased them about how many children they should have. It was a happy occasion and Jean Marc was glad to be there surrounded by so much love and happiness.

The men soon got out their fiddles and guitars and accordions and began to play. One of them asked Jean Marc if he had brought his fiddle and he laughed and told them that he was a bit out of practice but would work on it and maybe help them out the next time they got together.

Marguerite and Paul held hands and led the wedding march around the clearing and then the guests all surrounded the bride and groom as they danced their first dance together as man and wife. The pretty young girl looked up at her new husband with eyes shining with love and hope for the future. Marguerite's parents looked on with tears in their eyes. Jean Marc watched his friends and neighbors and hummed the song. That small clearing held couples who had been married for years, who witnessed the scene with smiles as they remembered the vows they had taken, while couples who hoped to marry soon observed with anticipation as they daydreamed about making vows of their own. Weddings brought happiness to most everyone, it seemed.

Jean Marc gave the bride the music box after the dance and she squealed with joy.

"Oh Jean Marc, it is so pretty. I love the song it plays...I think that it is called 'Claire de Lune.' I heard that played by a fancy orchestra on the radio."

"That is the name of the song, *Sha*, and I hope that you enjoy it. You look so beautiful today. That Paul is a lucky man. I hope that the two of you live a long and happy life together. "

She smiled up at him and said ", "Thank you, Jean Marc. I am sorry about what happened with you and Amy. My mama said that she was not the right girl for you and you will find someone else."

Jean Marc replied, "My mama says the same thing, *Sha*.

It just wasn't meant to be, I guess. I am doing OK and I have faith. It will all turn out right in the end."

He reached over to the small glass bowl on the nearby table and got himself a straight pin and then used it to pin a $5 bill to her veil, and they danced to the song in the music box.

The other guests also pinned money to Marguerite's dress and veil and to Paul's suit for dances, to give them plenty of money to start out their new life. No one had a lot to give, but every little bit helped.

And since Paul's older brother, Michel, was still single, he danced with a broom to show that he was still available and his mother loudly announced that it was because she wanted some good woman to take him off her hands and sweep him right out of her house. Everyone laughed at that even if they had heard the same joke many times before. Someone had tied a pretty sunbonnet on the head of the broom. Michel, another natural comedian, put on quite a show dipping and spinning his broom partner and making everyone laugh even more. He got so caught up in the game that he even stabbed the broomstick onto his toe to pretend that the broom had stepped on his foot. It was all in fun and there was a lot of playful ribbing and laughter as the young people called out to one another, "Hey, Michel, your girlfriend is too skinny," or "Hey Michel, you finally got yourself a blonde"…and then the band stuck up their rendition of the old Cajun song, "Jolie Blonde." As the night grew darker, the bride and groom were finally escorted down the road to the cabin where they would live together as man and wife. There was even more joking and teasing.

"Hey, Marguerite," Boo yelled out, "if that new husband of yours disappoints you, you let me know and I will be glad to take his place." Boo's wife, Marie, was pregnant and hit him on the arm for saying such a thing. Everyone laughed and reminded Boo that he was taken.

Marguerite blushed and shyly hid her face in her husband's neck as her groom carried her over the threshold of their new home. When the door was closed on the young couple, there were always a few of the group who would not let things go and banged on pots and pans and sang naughty songs they made up, to keep them awake in a "shivaree" while the rest of the group went back to the party to drink and dance and finish the good food.

Although Marguerite's mother had felt that the shivaree was more suited to a widow or older bride but was in poor taste for her innocent young daughter, she knew that no one meant anything bad by their pranks and it was all in fun and done with love for the newlyweds, so she chose not to become overly upset by it. They got caught up in the spirit of things and sometimes got a little carried away. She had to admit that some of the jokes they made were pretty funny and eventually she had laughed as hard as the rest of them.

Jean Marc and his friends stood together under the branches of a hundred-year-old oak tree sipping their drinks and talking about the day. Jean Marc wanted to catch up on all the happenings of his friends and neighbors over the past few years. But they all wanted to hear from him about what sounded to them like a big adventure. Some of them began asking him about his experiences during the war and it made him feel melancholy. Even though he understood their curiosity, he was not anxious to trade his upbeat mood for topics that were sure to make him have bad thoughts. There was no way he could explain his experiences to these people, most of whom had never been more than thirty miles from home in their whole lives. Young Phillip Robin had even asked if he knew for sure that he had killed anyone. Phillip was a child and meant nothing by it, but it brought bad thoughts to the front of Jean Marc's mind.

He did not want to think or talk about the things he had seen and he certainly did not want to talk about the things he had done. They had no idea what they were asking. He looked around at the wide questioning eyes of his old friends and felt nauseated. The faces of his fallen comrades would likely haunt him for years to come, and it almost felt like he was being disrespectful to discuss any of it. He had come here hoping for a rest from thinking. He tried very hard not to think about those things at all. He closed his eyes and saw Eric's face again in his mind, as he had so often. Eric laying there in a muddy foxhole beside the German soldier who resembled him so closely that they could have been brothers. It was too disturbing to think about right now. This was supposed to be a happy day.

Seeing so many of his family members here together, he also was reminded of the fact that he would have had a wedding himself if his girl had waited for him to return as he had hoped. Amy and Pierre had moved a few miles away to Breaux Bridge to live on Pierre's uncle's place to farm.

No, he didn't want to think about any of that. He tried to change the topic of discussion several times and when his efforts failed, he begged off, saying that he needed a bathroom break.

He walked back into the darkness to relieve his bladder. While standing farther downstream on the riverbank behind the bushes, so that he could not be seen, he looked into the darkness trying to clear his mind, then gazed back at the crowd and spotted Pierre and Amy standing at the far edge of the firelight. It was the first time he had seen them since his homecoming. It hurt a little to see them together but not as much as he had expected. From this distance, he could see them differently. Even he had to admit that they made a nice-looking couple. They looked happy. Pierre had his arms wrapped around Amy and she was leaning back into his chest. A certain dark inner part of his mind wanted to go over there and confront them and make a scene. He wanted to ask Amy what he had done to cause her to break her promise to wait for him. Seeing them together made him feel strange inside. They looked like a normal married couple. That was not what he had expected. He had expected raging anger and all he felt was a dull ache and empty feeling in his heart.

He lit up a Lucky Strike cigarette and took a deep drag. He let the smoke fill his lungs and waited for the nicotine lift.

Jean Marc looked up to the stars and thought of the nights he had looked at these stars when he was away from home and found comfort in knowing that the same blanket of stars covered both where he stood as well as his beloved here at home. Seeing her, there with her husband, made him sad and sick at heart. He was not angry at all. He should have realized that Amy and her husband would be there after all...it was their home too. The two of them had grown up with Marguerite and Paul the same as him. They looked content. It was time for him to finally accept the fact that his life was now heading off into another direction. The problem was that he didn't know where the new path would take him. It wasn't the first time that he had tried an unfamiliar trail, but those first few steps were always a little uncertain.

A bit beyond the trees, he saw a silver streak of light with a fiery tail shooting downward and disappearing below the level of the treetops. He glanced back at his friends to see if any of them had seen the same sight. But they were so involved in their own activities that he knew they had not noticed the silver streak. They were laughing and telling stories and enjoying the chance to be together. The dancing couples didn't notice anything but the music and each other. The older women were doing their kitchen chores and talking together and did not appear to have seen anything unusual either. The men were deep in their cups and were telling the same old stories to one another that they always told at gatherings like this one.

At that point, he realized that his party mood was gone and he wanted to go home. He took one last drag from the Lucky Strike and then thumped the cigarette butt out into the water. He heard a little hiss when it landed and then the red glow disappeared.

He limped over to his mother and kissed her on the forehead, saying, "Mama, my leg is bothering me some and I am heading back to my own place to go to bed."

She sympathetically patted him on the cheek, replying, "All right, *Sha*, you go on home and get some rest, yeah. Do you need anything?"

"No, Mama, I will be fine, I've just been running around a lot the past few days and I guess I need to rest some. I'm all right. I will see you tomorrow."

His leg was not bothering him much at all, but he knew that if his mother thought that it was hurting him, she would not question his leaving early and would cover for him if any of the others noticed his absence.

He hated to play mind-games like that, but sometimes it was simpler to play a little game or tell a little white lie than to try to explain the truth. He wasn't even sure that he could explain the truth at this point and if he did, they were unlikely to understand it any better than he did. This strange but wonderful day had left him with a vague kind of empty feeling. He needed something to fill his heart and make it sing again.

CHAPTER
TWENTY-SIX

L ife was more complicated now than it used to be. Until he was hurt, he had never had the time to give a lot of thought to things that he now labeled as "feelings." Most of his life had been spent reacting to whatever happened in his life, but not in analyzing his reactions to those happenings. After his injuries, he had a lot of time to spend lying in a hospital bed. The doctors and nurses came in and out of the room taking his temperature or blood pressure and they were always asking him how he felt about one thing or another. He never knew what to tell them. He was brought up to believe a man does not talk about his feelings. The only times he remembered his father talking about feelings were if he was angry about something or was making a joke. The medical people insisted that it was important for him to tell them his feelings, so that they could help him. He didn't see much sense in complaining that his leg hurt or that he wished his friends had not died. He didn't see how telling them that he had not had a letter from Amy in over a year would help either. Talking was not going to fix any of those things. So he did what he had to do to get better and marked each day as one day closer to his being able to go home. In his world, there were always things that needed to be done, regardless of how a person felt about doing the jobs. It took a while for him to figure out how he felt about things. But he was slowly working it all out one thought at a time.

He stood in his pirogue and pushed away from the bank with the long pole to head downstream to go home. He waved goodbye to his friends and left them there to party as late as they wanted. This whole week had been full of stress and strain and he found suddenly that he was looking forward to sleep. He let the current take him slowly on his way and looked out into the darkness.

He saw the shining yellow eyes of a big alligator a moment before the gator sank almost silently into the swirling muddy water. There were plenty of gators in this swampy place, but most of the time they left humans alone unless the gators were very large or very hungry. Seeing the gator made him think of their textured hides that made nice boots and pocketbooks and luggage and would put a lot of good money in his coffee can to use for his new automobile. Maybe he and Boo ought to set up a hunt one of these nights soon and see how many they could get. While he was distracted, he almost passed his turn and had to push his pole into the deep mud to keep from going the wrong way.

He laughed at himself and said aloud, "Dis here *bateau* done forgot the way home."

His eye caught a movement on the bank and saw the little pale man-thing again. He was standing behind a bush but he was much closer than the other time he had seen him. His bald head was shaped almost like an egg with the pointed end as a chin and he had no hair. His eyes were very large and dark and shiny. His skin was ghostly white, like he never spent any time in the sun. He almost glowed. He was wearing a shiny-looking suit that appeared to be made in one piece. Jean Marc was not sure what to do, so he did the usual thing anyone on the water would do...he raised one hand as a way of saying hello to anyone they saw standing on the bank as they went by. The little man hesitated a few seconds and then slowly raised his hand in the same fashion. The boat passed the site and Jean Marc almost lost his balance from looking back to watch for as long as he could.

He had seen people from Japan and Africa and Greece and Arabia and many other parts of the world, but none of them resembled this stranger.

There was a trace of fear in his mind as he asked himself if he believed that this man could be from somewhere out there for real...meaning out there in space. It shook his faith and made him feel uneasy to even consider that. He had run through these swamps his entire life and never seen anything like that guy before.

If he is a spaceman, then why is he here?

And what does he want?

Should we be afraid?

Is he the only one or are there more of them hiding out somewhere?

His mind was racing as the questions rolled around inside his head. The truth was that he wanted to turn around and go back and see the man-thing and find the answers to his questions. He didn't feel fear nearly as much as he felt curiosity.

Or maybe I had more scuppernong wine at the wedding than I thought I did. He ran his hand through his hair and growled deep inside his chest from sheer frustration. He wished that he could switch off his brain and make the thinking stop for a while. *Maybe I am shell-shocked,* he thought to himself. *Maybe a lot of things...maybe anything but seeing a pale little man from outer space.*

Damn! I know what I saw and I want to know more about them, but I am afraid of finding out something that would be really scary. The little man doesn't look very scary to me, he thought. *But how would we know? He has not made any threatening moves, but then I don't know if he has a weapon and what he could do if he wanted to hurt me. He could shoot fire out of his fingertips for all I know.*

The enemy sometimes looks exactly like the rest of us. That German soldier certainly looked a lot like Eric and now both of them are dead. Am I making a mistake by not reporting this to someone in authority? But who would I report it to? I don't want to cause a problem for the spaceman if he is here for peaceful purposes, but I also don't want to go to the sheriff and report that there are spacemen here and look like a fool when they come looking for a man in a silver suit and find nothing. His family would be embarrassed and he would be humiliated. Sheriff Bertrand had been sheriff for over twenty years and Jean Marc knew for a fact that he would laugh in his face if he told him about this pale man-thing in a silver suit that flies an aircraft that looks like a shooting star as it leaves or enters our nighttime sky.

CHAPTER
TWENTY-SEVEN

Jean Marc had a restless night. He had vivid dreams of shells exploding and his friends' dead faces and silver-suited spacemen dancing with Amy at a wedding. His bed was soaked with sweat when his eyes popped open before sunrise. He lay there listening to the night sounds for a while longer, hoping to doze again. It didn't work, so he finally decided that he might as well get up. He was fully awake and there were chores to be done. He let Chili go outside to do his doggy business while he made his first pot of coffee for this day. He put a couple of eggs on to boil and split a couple of Mama's leftover biscuits to toast in the black iron skillet.

He had a plan. Today, after he checked his traps and skinned out the catch, he was going to town. He needed to buy more salt to cure the hides. He also wanted to speak to Boo and Elloi about a gator hunt. The more he thought about it, the more he looked forward to it. It had been a long time since he and his friends were out in the swamp together. He missed the camaraderie of the old days. He guessed that it would be good for all of them.

Gator hunting was dangerous, for sure, but it was exciting too. Night hunting for frogs and gators and even possums or raccoons was always an adventure. A good gator hunt was exactly what he needed to pull him out of this strange mood and get him focused again. Something was bound to happen that would provide storytelling material for years to come. He could also get some meat for good eatin'. He had an almost empty smokehouse and could not expect his parents to feed him forever. The frog legs were delicious cooked in butter and garlic and the gator tail meat was tasty too. At least, it was good the way his mama cooked it with a spicy sauce piquant. The swamp was one big grocery store if you knew where to look and what to do with whatever you harvested.

There was an old joke about the difference between a zoo in the big cities in the North and a Cajun zoo. In the North they would have a sign by the cage that tells you the name of the animal and where it comes from. If there ever was a Cajun zoo, they would probably have a sign by the cages that would tell you the name of the animal and where it comes from and also...the recipe. Jean Marc had never been to a zoo, but he could imagine the animals in cages for the public to see. The idea of locking up wild animals bothered him a little. It was like putting animals in prison, when they hadn't done anything except be what they are: wild animals. But maybe his thinking came from living wild and free with the animals here in his own part of the world. He would not want to be locked up in a zoo, so he could not imagine that an animal would like it much either.

He hurried through his chores and cleaned up before heading to the store. His two friends, Elloi and Boo, and also Boo's pretty little wife Marie were there when he went in to get himself a few groceries. The guys got all excited about his idea of a night hunt. They agreed to split the money for the alligator hides the same as they had in years past. They would all help with the work and all of them wanted to go tonight. They had not been gator hunting in a very long time, so they welcomed the idea and they all felt there was no sense in waiting. It would be like the good old days. Mr. Landry laughed about it. He figured they had all forgotten how it was done. He said that if he was a betting man, he would put his money on the gators tonight.

Boo said that even if they didn't get a gator, he needed a night away from Marie. She playfully hit him on the shoulder and made him agree to get her some frog legs if she let him go out to play with his friends. Her third baby was overdue and she was very uncomfortable, maybe even a bit grumpy, but she said that some frog legs cooked in garlic and butter might make her feel better. She was standing there, lovingly rubbing her bulging belly and giving him a sweet, flirty-wife look that he could not resist, so he told her that he would try. Boo said he would take Marie and the two baby-girls over to her mama's house while they were out, so that they would not be at home alone since the new baby could come at any time now.

CHAPTER
TWENTY-EIGHT

They spent the rest of the day getting their equipment ready. They dug around in Boo's storage shed where it had all been stored since Jean Marc had left for the Army. Boo said he had not gone night hunting a single time while Jean Marc was gone. There hadn't seemed to be any point. It had always been something the three of them did as a team. Now that the team was back together, it was time to go.

The three of them dug through the storehouses like dogs digging up a bone. Everything was exactly where they had put it after the last hunt, years ago. They were glad to have hard hats with carbide lamps to help them see in the dark. They had to take lengths of chain and rope and big hooks and heavy gloves. They also had tall, thick rubber boots to help protect from snake bites as well as keep their feet dry.

Boo's papa said that behind the outhouse out back was a bucket full of chicken heads and innards from when they killed some for a gumbo the day before. He had taken the stuff out there to find a place to bury it, but then they had company drop by the house and he had not gotten the job done yet. By now it should be good and stinky.

Boo was taking his old truck to hold the catch. They were hoping for a big one or even more than one. He used a small file to sharpen the deadly points of his frog gigs, which resembled small sharply barbed forks on long poles, and found a couple of big buckets in case they found a good place to get some frogs. If his Marie was craving frog's legs then Boo was going to please her if he could, although the frogs were not his biggest reason for going. The whole idea was exciting to them, but it was also serious business and they had to be ready for whatever might happen.

The main thing they were hoping to find tonight was the gators. Jean Marc brought along his 12-gauge shotgun as a precaution. Being out in the swamp at night could be dangerous. Elloi had a 30/30 lever action Winchester, so they were feeling pretty much ready for anything.

The three friends had spent their late teen years perfecting their own method of catching alligators. They used to be pretty good at it, but that was a few years ago and they all expected this hunt was not going to go as smoothly as the ones in the past. Mr. Landry was probably right about that part. It didn't matter. It was good to be back together again and doing the things they used to do. All three of them were giddy with excitement and glad to be there.

Some of the gator hunters used meat on a big heavy iron hook to hook the big animals, almost like catching a very big fish, and then as they hauled it into the boat, they would club it over the head or shoot it to subdue the animal. Boo and Elloi and Jean Marc had decided that was too messy and too much hard work. They had come up with their own way of doing things and it had proven to be successful and a whole lot less messy and less dangerous too in their way of thinking. It might not be the way to work for someone who caught gators on a regular basis for a living because they had to stay close to the roads where they could take the truck, but for the kind of occasional hunting that they did, it worked out fine and they had a lot of fun doing it.

First they would take an old burlap sack and put a bunch of chicken innards and heads in it and tie it up tight. Alligators seemed to like chicken better than anything. They tied that sack to the end of a long rope. They tied the other end of the rope to the trailer hitch on the back of Boo's old Ford truck. Then they picked a good spot. All three of them knew this swamp like the back of their own hands but each had his favorite spot in mind. There was usually a bit of wrangling before they settled on the exact place, but they enjoyed that part too. They backed the truck down as close to the water as they felt was safe and stopped. Elloi had the best throwing arm, so he would toss the stinky bait as far out in the water as he could and then they would sit quietly and wait. It was a smelly process, with the nasty juice from the sack getting on everything. The gator would smell the stinky stuff and grab hold of the sack in the water and start to do barrel rolls over and over under the water. They would then pull him onto the land with the truck, or by hand if he wasn't too big, but tonight they wanted a big one. They would get the beast up on land and tie a rope around his snout so he couldn't open his mouth. The old folks said an alligator has fewer and weaker mouth-opening muscles than he has mouth-closing ones, so he is easier to control if he keeps his mouth shut.

Boo would always say that idea reminds him of his wife,

but he wouldn't say it within her range of hearing. It was an old joke and besides, she claimed to swing a mean rolling pin when sufficiently riled. Boo claimed right back that the bigger her belly got, the more easily riled she became. No one else was ready to put her to the test. Boo also already knew for sure that her pretty brown eyes could glow red like hot coals when she got angry. Maybe he would take home that bucket of frog legs for her after all. It might go a long way toward getting him out of the doghouse for drinking too much homemade wine at the wedding the other night. Besides that, he felt sorry for her being so big and so miserable while waiting for this baby to come. He hoped that the baby would be born soon, so that Marie would feel better and also because a new little one was an exciting thing. Nine months is a long time to wait for a new member of the family. Boo loved his wife dearly and enjoyed his family and was excited about being a father again.

Elloi picked up the bag of stinky bait and threatened to make a big production of winding up like a baseball pitcher but didn't. Boo and Jean Marc had begged, "Nooooooo, Elloi, don't do it." They would have all gotten spattered with smelly juice, so he lobbed the bag of stinky chicken parts as far out into the muddy water as he could, where it made a big splash. That was good. It alerted the gator population that some animal might have fallen into the water. With luck they would come around to investigate and the trio would get their hides pretty quick.

Boo said, "If things go well, two or three will come at one time. We could load up the truck all in one trip, yeah. More than that could get kind of scary, but we could handle a couple of them, don't you think?" They all laughed and grinned at each other. That scariness was part of the mix and provided storytelling material for later. Sometimes the retelling of the tale was more exciting than the actual adventure, but that was OK too. Sometimes they got overtaken by their sense of adventure and wished for more than they could handle.

They sat in the back of the truck and smoked their hand-rolled cigarettes and talked quietly while they waited. It gave them time to catch up a little. Elloi was getting restless and was talking about moving to Lafayette or Baton Rouge to find work. He had been fishing and shrimping for most of his adult life and was finding it harder and harder to sell his fish and shrimp.

He said, "Jean Marc, you know how it is? I want to see what is out there in the world instead of spending the rest of my life in Butte La Rose, Louisiana."

Jean Marc told him, "Don't sell this place short, Elloi, I am glad to be back in Butte La Rose, Louisiana, me. I am goin' to sell my skins and do OK. I don't want to go someplace else to work."

CHAPTER TWENTY-NINE

The eight-foot bull gator didn't give them too much time to talk about it. He glided silently into view and dove down to grab the bag of chicken in his toothy jaws. The water was whipped into a muddy froth as he rolled over and over trying to drown his prey. Boo jumped up front, put the truck into gear and slowly pulled forward. The gator was pulled right up onto the river bank, thanks to his stubborn refusal to let go of his stinky treasure. Jean Marc and Elloi ran down to tie a rope around the gator's snout, but the wily gator let go of the bag and took a step back. He looked at each of them with his mean yellow eyes and opened his mouth wide and hissed at them angrily. Neither of the guys was eager to wrestle a gator out there in the mud, so Elloi reached into the back of the truck and grabbed a baseball bat to hit him in the head, but the old gator managed to slip backwards into the water and disappear before they could get close enough to dispatch him.

They all laughed about being a little out of practice and decided to find another place. They punched each other's arms and teased about who did what wrong with their first hunt.

Elloi kept chastising himself and saying, "I should'a just pulled out my gun and shot him. I don't know why

I didn't just shoot him in the head. That wouldn't have hurt the hide. Poooyieeee...we are sho-nuff out of practice, fellas. Boo, your papa was right. Maybe we should'a made us some bets with Aaron and at least we'd a gotten some money out of the deal."

Jean Marc told Elloi, "Well now, Ole Man Gator there is goin' to tell all his gator friends that we are here, so we need to go up toward your papa's house and try in that little cove with the willow trees, don't you think?"

They threw the ropes and the wet sack of stinky chicken in the truck bed and headed down the almost invisible path. Boo was singing a song that he had been singing for years, with words that changed to suit his mood and circumstances, but the tune was always the same. Jean Marc smiled to himself as he heard Boo singing something like

Ole man gator done got his self away tonight
but we'll get him next time in da pale moonlight.

"Boo Landry, Cajun poet and songwriter," he joked. They all laughed together. It was fun being out here in the dark with his friends again after so long, and none of them cared if they got a gator or not.

There had been a time years ago when they had shared a good many nights like this. Going out tonight had been a good idea and he was feeling close to his friends again. It seemed as though all three were feeling that way.

"Boo, shut that racket, up, you are going to scare away the gators for sure," Elloi hollered from the back of the truck. He was using a voice three times louder than Boo's singing. They all laughed and Boo kept on singing only louder, this time.

Elloi asked, "Did y'all hear about that guy at the store yesterday? He was lookin' for men to work in the oil field. He put up a paper on the wall to tell where to go to fill out an application for work. I am thinking on it. They're paying good money, heck of a lot more than I am getting sitting here on my butt, listening to Boo serenade the frogs and gators," laughed Elloi.

The other two didn't say much. Jean Marc might look into it, but Boo had a baby on the way and a fat paycheck was kind of interesting, even if he was not thrilled with the idea of having a real job that involved schedules and taking orders from bosses and such.

They rounded a bend and spotted another place where the bank sloped gently into the muddy water. The water lilies were floating in a green raft for six or more feet across the water. The smell of the night-blooming flowers was delicious.

Boo said, "It seems a shame to stink up this pretty smelling place with rotten chicken guts, don't it yeah?"

Elloi agreed, but threw the stinky bag into the water anyway. It made a good loud splash, so all they had to do next was wait to see if any gators came to investigate the noise.

Boo got his frog gigs and buckets out of the truck bed and took himself off to one side and down the bank to a likely place to find bull frogs. It was not long at all before he had enough in his buckets to make a nice dinner for the family, and he put his gear back in the truck and joined his friends in the gator-watching vigil. As the time passed slowly the talk drifted from subject to subject. Elloi asked

Jean Marc about the foreign women he had seen and was disappointed that he had not left a string of broken hearts all over Europe. They covered about every other topic worth pursuing and some that weren't worth it but they talked about them anyway. By that time, Boo had begun to sing again and they were running out of Prince Albert cigarette tobacco. Eventually they gave up the idea of getting a big one and were ready to head on back home. Evidently Old Man Gator had spread the word and no one in the gator community was interested in chicken tonight. They dumped the stinky mess on the muddy bank figuring that after they left, some animal would come along and get the tasty snack. If they took it home, then Boo would likely be the one who had to bury the stuff, so it was just as well that they fed it to the wildlife. They climbed into the truck and headed back toward home. Although they had not gotten a gator, it didn't matter. They spent time together and renewed their feelings of closeness, which mattered a lot more than getting an alligator. They would have plenty of years to hunt gators together.

Jean Marc leaned out the window to see if the gators had come to collect their offering. It would be so like one of those big ones to show up now that the hunt was called off. The small silvery man was kicking at the offal with the toe of his shiny boot. He looked at Jean Marc and raised his hand in a wave and Jean Marc put his hand down below the level of the window so that Boo and Elloi would not see and waved back to him. *That little guy sure does get around,* he thought to himself. He was beginning to accept the fact that the little man was real and that he was not crazy. He was still very curious and wondered how to find out more about the spaceman and how to get to know him better. He wished there was a way to say hello other than only a wave. The whole idea was less scary now than it was that first morning and his curiosity was growing every day.

CHAPTER THIRTY

They got back to Marie's parents' house and found a lot of activity. The baby was coming. Marie was in the final stages of a quick and hard labor. Her papa was sitting at the kitchen table drinking coffee and waiting with worry in his eyes. Marie's mama was doing midwife duty. Judging by the loud moaning and screaming noises coming from the bedroom, the birth was imminent.

Marie's papa welcomed the guys back from the gator hunt and offered them coffee. That way all the men could sit in the kitchen looking white-faced and uncomfortable while the women and Mother Nature did the birthing thing in the back room. Men were not allowed in there until it was over.

Jean Marc got himself a cup of coffee and sat down at the kitchen table with the rest of the men to wait it out. Every few minutes Marie's mama would come out and give someone an order. She sent Jean Marc out to the shed to get another wash tub for dirty linens. Marie's papa was pouring a big kettle of hot water into another laundry tub right now, so that they could wash off the baby and give Marie a wash-up when it was done. Boo was praying that Marie was going to be all right and at the end of his prayer, he added that he hoped for a boy this time. He had two precious little girls but was seriously hoping that this time was going be different. Marie's papa told him to quit fretting.

Boo was upset with himself. He felt guilty that he had been out chasing gators and his wife was here having the baby. He felt like he should have been here instead of chasing around through the swamp with his friends. Every moan and scream ate at his conscience and left him feeling helpless and sad.

His mother-in-law told him, "Son, get yourself some coffee and quit worrying about it. There was not one blessed thing that you could have done here. Marie would have rather had you out there with Jean Marc and Elloi than have you hovering around here and getting in the way, especially when it was going slow. It is going to be over here in a few minutes anyway. She is built like me and has babies easy. It is all going to be OK, so quit worrying over it."

Marie gave a loud growl that turned into a shriek that ripped through the house like a big wind and then stopped suddenly. It sounded painful. The men all looked at one another with white faces and gave a silent prayer of thanks that men don't have to go through that. If that was having babies easy, then none of them wanted to see what it was like to do it hard. Marie yelled for her mama and immediately her mother hurried back to see what was happening. A few short minutes later, they heard the sweet soft cry of a newborn baby.

Marie's papa wiped the tears from his eyes and grinned at them all, holding his coffee cup up in the air and making a toast. "That little sound could melt the coldest heart," he said. Then they all made the sign of the cross and said a silent prayer to thank God that the baby was here and that everything was OK. All of them had tears in their eyes, but no one mentioned it. It was an accepted fact that the coffee must have been too hot.

A few minutes later, Marie's mama brought a tightly wrapped bundle out to show them. Boo had gotten his boy. The tiny red face peeked out of its blanket and everyone crowded around to catch a look. The dark little eyes were shining brightly as the newest Landry gazed back at the bigger faces looking him over. Jean Marc uncovered the tiny fist and stroked the fingers. The little hand wrapped around his finger and squeezed it more tightly than Jean Marc would have thought was possible from a brand-new baby. This was a strong little fellow and that was good. He would need to be strong to live in this world of uncertainty.

Jean Marc laughed and said, "Hey dere T-Boo...*Sha Bébé...Bienvenu*e, welcome to the world."

Boo took his new son carefully into his arms and went in to be with his wife. He was very happy. He felt very blessed. Marie was smiling as she took her son to her breast and saw the love in her husband's eyes as he sat there beside her. They were a family. The two little girls would wake up to find that they had a new baby brother while they were sleeping. The older one would be a big help to her mother. The younger daughter would find that she was no longer the baby and would have to share her mother's attention a little more but would soon adjust.

CHAPTER
THIRTY-ONE

The sky was still dark and cloudy when Jean Marc left Boo's house and walked the two miles back to his own home. His mind was full of longing. He wanted a family of his own. The air was cool and the misty devil's breath was hovering barely above the ground and the water. Chili was sitting there waiting for him by the porch like always. He sat down on the top step to pet the dog and ponder a bit. Jean Marc had been thinking about the way life worked out. He sadly considered once again that if Amy had not married Pierre, that they might be married by now and planning for their own family. Then he realized that Amy was already starting her family. She and Pierre were living his dream of a life together. Maybe that was OK.

"Life doesn't always follow the plans we make, that's for sure," he told Chili as he rubbed his dog's knobby head and looked out across the water. He half expected to see the little shiny man-thing out there somewhere, but he didn't see anything out of the ordinary. He did hear the grunt of the big ole gator who lived down the way a bit, but he had heard that sound so often that it was almost a comfort somehow, so he went in to wash up and try to get some sleep. He could not help but wonder if that old gator was the same one they saw tonight. That old man had been living there for as long as he could remember.

He thought about having a dose of the Hadacol but decided that he was so tired that he didn't have the energy to get up and get it. He washed up as quickly as he could without even heating the water first and threw himself into his bed.

As soon as he began to doze, he was awakened by Chili's loud barking. The dog was using the same kind of excited barking that he had used the night he got into it with that big ole raccoon so many years before. The very tone of it said that something was seriously wrong. Jean Marc reached down to the floor and grabbed his rifle from under the edge of the bed where he kept it and hit the floor running in one smooth motion wearing nothing but his GI underwear. He had lost so much that was near to his heart the past couple of years and he was not about to lose that old dog too...not if he could help it, anyway. He went out the front door of the house and yelled the dog's name as he jumped off the porch and landed in the soft mud on his way to the docks. He could see Chili had something in his sights and was raising Cain about it, but wasn't actively in a fight with it, and that was a relief. Getting closer let him see that the big gator from around the curve was rolling in the water not far from the bank and whatever it had caught was fighting hard to get away. Jean Marc looked closer and realized with a sudden shock that the gator had caught the silver man-thing and was doing a good job of dragging him deeper into the water. Jean Marc took aim at the gator and let off a shot, trying hard to not hit the shiny man. He missed. He was being too cautious. He tried again. He missed. He was letting his emotions get in the way. He had to take time to get it right.

He took a deep breath to calm his nerves. The third shot did the trick. He saw the gator go limp and start to sink. Jean Marc grabbed a tie-up rope off the nail driven into a tree stump and splashed into the cool water up to his knees to try to grab the gator some way. He managed to grab the silver man's boot and used it to pull him and the gator up to the bank. He was then able to pry open the jaws and carefully take the man out of the animal's mouth. The silver man's eyes were open but he hadn't said a word or made a sound. Jean Marc laid him down on the bank and tried to examine him as much as he could. He felt his neck and found there was a strong but rapid pulse. That pulse made it all the more real to him and it made the silver man seem more normal somehow. Finally, he scooped the small man up in his arms like a child and took him inside the house, all the while muttering prayers and asking God's mercy on this little man from so far away. He gently laid him on the couch and ran to the kitchen sink. Jean Marc asked him over and over, "You all right?…Do you hurt anywhere? Are you bleeding?"

Jean Marc got a clean damp wash rag and carefully cleaned him up the best he could and then looked at him. He didn't know what else to do. Generally speaking, he looked a lot like a human being. The silvery-looking suit was a suit and not a part of his body and was not torn anyplace. There seemed to be no blood or even any scratches as far as Jean Marc could tell. It was fascinating to see this man-thing up close, but he did not know what to say or what language to say it in, so he rocked back on his heels and blinked his eyes and smiled. He was calmer now, but felt kind of silly sitting there grinning like an idiot. He couldn't help but wonder what the silver-suited man was thinking.

The stranger's large dark eyes blinked once and then the man slowly reached out his pale-skinned hands with long slender fingers, softly touching Jean Marc on both temples at once. At first, Jean Marc was afraid. He could feel his own heart racing. What was this thing going to do to him? Was it safe to allow this person to touch him? The silver man closed his big eyes and as if by magic, Jean Marc heard the words inside his head.

"Thank you, Jean Marc Thibodaux, you are a good soldier. I am called Sacam. I am also a soldier and a scientist and explorer, but I am not at war. I will not harm you. Do you understand?"

Jean Marc was amazed. He nodded his head slowly and rocked back on his heels again. This time, his smile was genuine.

Sacam nodded his own head and spoke into Jean Marc's mind again. "I thank you again for saving me from that powerful creature. I must go now." He stood up quickly and almost took a step, but shakily fell back toward the couch again.

Jean Marc reached out to steady him and helped to get him seated again. Sacam thanked him for his support and asked if he might be allowed to remain there for a short time to regain his strength.

Jean Marc found himself answering in his mind without

speaking the words aloud, and told Sacam that he was welcome to stay for as long as he felt that he needed to. And the strange part was that he meant it. Here he was, communicating with the strangest being that he had ever seen in his whole life, and he felt right at ease with him like they were old friends.

Sacam said, "Thank you for your kindness," and stretched his legs out to lie flat on the sofa. He sighed softly and blinked his large dark eyes. It was obvious that his encounter with the alligator had shaken him up a bit. An incident with a big alligator was enough to shake anyone up a bit and then some.

Jean Marc asked if he would like help to remove the boots so that he would be more comfortable. Sacam nodded, reached down with one slender hand, and pulled on the front edge and the boots came apart without a zipper or buckles or anything. There were strips of some kind of tape that joined the two pieces together in the front. Jean Marc tried not to stare at the bare feet that were shaped much like human feet, but when he had removed the stockings that covered them, Jean Marc could see that the long pale toes were loosely joined together, not like a duck exactly but like human toes with thin webs of skin between each one. The skin was milky white with no markings or hair of any kind. It looked as smooth as marble but felt soft and warm to the touch, much like his own human skin. He looked up to see Sacam watching him. Jean Marc was embarrassed at being caught staring, but Sacam told him in his mind that it was right and normal to be curious. He said that he also was curious about their differences. He reached out one hand

and touched the skin of Jean Marc's arm. He stroked the dark hair covering the skin and muttered, "Amazing."

Jean Marc laughed and told him, "My mama always told me I was part bear."

Sacam looked confused. He said, "A bear is a very large hairy animal? Your mother thinks you are part bear? That is not possible."

Jean Marc laughed.

Jean Marc told Sacam to rest. He then walked over and closed the front door, leaving Chili looking very puzzled there on the porch. Then he lay down in his own bed, but put his rifle within reach in case something else were to happen. This had been a very long day. And he closed his eyes to sleep.

The bright morning sun woke him up, which was rather unusual. Jean Marc was a very early riser by habit, but he must have needed some extra sleep after all the excitement of the night before. Glancing over to see if Sacam was still asleep as well, he saw that the sofa was empty.

CHAPTER THIRTY-TWO

As was his habit, he got up to make himself a pot of coffee and went outside on the back porch to say Good Morning to the world and to take a leak off the side of the porch while looking around to see what there was to see. Chili was nosing around the bushes in a normal way and the air was already warming up. He glanced at his watch and saw that it was already after seven am. He mentally chastised himself for sleeping later than he should have. After getting dressed, he went out the front door heading to his boat.

There on the dock was the dead body of that old gator. It was a beautiful animal. The hide was marked with a distinct pattern and the color was even and rich with no blemishes. In all likelihood that old gator had been in this swamp for more years than Jean Marc had been alive. It was a shame to see him gone, but under the circumstances, there had been no choice. He couldn't have stood there and let the gator eat the small man in the silver suit. Sometimes there are tough decisions that have to be made. There was the bullet hole that he had put in it himself, but it was in a place that would not affect the price of the skin, and he was grinning as he imagined the amount he might get to add to his coffee can before long. He pulled out his skinning knife and set to work. After the hide was prepared, he cut off a large section of the big meaty tail and carefully wrapped it in a sheet of oilcloth to take to his mother. Mama would know how to turn that cut of tough and stringy meat into a delicious meal, and it had been a long time since he had tasted alligator in sauce piquant. This large cut of meat would make a Sunday dinner to feed the whole Thibodaux family.

He wondered where Sacam was today and what he was doing out there in the swamp. It looked to Jean Marc as though he had himself a new friend. But he was not at all sure that he wanted to share the news of this new friendship with his family or neighbors yet. Somehow, he knew in his heart that they would not understand. His brother Aaron would be rounding up his old cronies and going out with guns to capture the spaceman. *No,* he thought, *some things were best kept to one's own self.*

Jean Marc went about his normal routine of fishing and tending his traps and hunting for squirrels or rabbits every day and saw Sacam doing his own routine of gathering and observing nature. They encountered each other in many odd places. Now that they were acquainted, there seemed to be no reason to hide from each other. Jean Marc enjoyed their conversations and looked for his friend every day when he worked. They took great pains to avoid being seen by anyone else, however. Jean Marc did not trust his own people's reactions if they discovered the existence of a being so different from themselves. Sacam told him that not being discovered was one of his most important rules.

His people were afraid that the Earth beings were not ready to accept the presence of others in the universe.

During one of these visits, Sacam told him, "I am going home tonight. I should return in a few of your Earth days. I have been coming here for several months. I collect specimens of plants and drawings or what you call photographs of insect life to take back home. My wife studies them and is putting together a book to be used by all space travelers. I have tried taking the animals themselves, but then I am concerned about what food they need and I have to return them to their own habitat. The cages take up a lot of space in my ship and I worry about their safety on the journey home and back. I don't like the idea of causing the death of any creature. "

Jean Marc thought that there were surely enough bugs in this world to spare a few for research but he appreciated Sacam's ideas about not killing things. It made him feel safer to think that Sacam's people were not likely to come to Earth as a military force.

Jean Marc asked, "Where is your home? How far away is it?"

Sacam pointed to the skies and told Jean Marc, "My planet is many hundreds of thousands of miles away in that direction. I have a machine in my aircraft that I program the coordinates into and the aircraft flies itself to those coordinates. That way, I can sleep during most of the trip. It takes me about a day and a half in Earth time to get there and the same to get back here. "

Jean Marc nodded his head. He did not understand the idea of an aircraft flying itself, but he was fascinated by the idea of Sacam traveling all those miles to come here to gather bugs and plants. The notion that there are others out there who come here to explore this planet is a strange one in some ways, but then he knew that there were scientists from here on our Earth who would gladly go to other planets to do those same things if they had the ability to do it. Now that he was getting to know Sacam a little more each time they visited together, it wasn't as difficult to imagine. He never had given a lot of thought to space or visitors from other planets before these strange incidents began to happen, but now he found the whole idea appealed to him. He thought about it a lot during his hours alone. He would look into the nighttime sky and wonder if the day would ever come when people from his own planet would go flying off to get specimens from another world. He hoped that it would happen. He wanted to go up there to see what was on the moon. But it was still not something he would ever bring up at the family supper table.

CHAPTER THIRTY-THREE

Jean Marc was skinning his catch late one morning when Sacam walked up to him and asked him inside his head, "Why are you doing this brutal thing to the animals? You do not always eat the flesh of this beast, so why do you take its life? I do not understand."

Jean Marc tried to explain. "Many people here on this world like wearing the fur of the animals for clothing. It is natural and the fur keeps them warm in the cold winter months. Even though the winter months are not so cold here, there are other parts of the country that get very cold and they need the fur coats. I catch the animals in these traps and skin them and sell the furs in order to make money to buy the things I need to live. I do eat some of the animals, like the nutria. It is a lot like a big rabbit and tastes a lot like that too. They are vegetarian. Some people eat the raccoon but I don't care for it much."

Sacam listened, but still seemed disturbed by the idea of it all. He said, "My people do not eat the flesh or wear the skins of animals...we create the fabrics that we need for clothing and for household use in factories. We do not kill our indigenous animals, because the Creator made them for his own purpose and we as a people chose not to kill any of the things our Creator made. The Creator came to our world once and gave us a set of rules to live by. One of the rules was 'Thou shall not kill.' My people took that literally and so we do not intentionally kill anything."

"What about Jesus? Do your people believe in Him too? He was the son of God and came here to show us the way back to heaven. He was sacrificed for our sins. If we believe in Jesus, then we accept him as our savior and are baptized, well, then we know that when we die, our spirits will go to heaven and be with God forever.

"I don't know about heaven or anyone called Jesus," Sacam told him. "We do have the lessons of The Creator's son named Hamon. He was a teacher who came to us to show us the way to live. He lived by example and taught my people that if we follow the laws left by His Father, the Creator, then our world would thrive and our people would be happy. He was not sacrificed as far as I know. He was a very good man and a great teacher who lived a long time ago and left us many books and letters for guidance. I do not know what will happen when I finally stop living. I suppose that will be part of the adventure...to see what comes next. But I choose to follow the rules and teachings of the Creator, and hope that the outcome is a good one."

"Does everyone there follow the rules?" Jean Marc asked. "It seems to me that it wouldn't work unless everyone did it."

"Yes, they do, because we learned a long time ago, many years before I was born, that things run more smoothly when everyone follows the same rules. My people are not very aggressive by nature, so they prefer the peace and quiet. There were times in the past when strangers came to our world and caused problems but usually they discovered that we have nothing on our world that would be useful to them and they eventually go away and leave us alone. We are not fighters. The stories say that the people would hide in caves when the strangers came."

Jean Marc could not begin to imagine a world where everyone followed the rules any more than he could imagine a world without eating his favorite meats. Even though it seemed that the peace and tranquility would be nice, there didn't seem to be much excitement on Sacam's world. Everyone looked the same and talked the same and nobody broke the rules. That seemed impossible and sounded very dull. It appeared to Jean Marc that all that peace and quiet came with a price of boredom. He also knew that if strangers came and tried to take what little his own people had, they would fight to the death to protect it. Hiding was not in their nature. That did answer one question, however; there must be other strangers out there who travel in the skies. Earth is not the only planet that is occupied. He wondered how the good folks from Earth would react to that bit of news.

Jean Marc asked, "What do your people eat for food if you don't eat the animals?" He had offered Sacam breakfast as well as other food over the time since they met but Sacam never even tasted anything that was offered.

Sacam said, "I don't think most of the foods that we eat exist here. The travel food that I brought with me here is a powder that I mix with water that I brought with me in bottles. I also have some little cakes. They are very nutritious. It is all made from our native plants. We do eat plants and prepare them in many ways but have not eaten animals for many of your centuries. There is more to it than not wanting to displease the Creator; the scientists found many years ago that the plant-based foods made the people healthier and so we grow or have created our own foods that are now eaten all over our planet. There may have been a time when animals were used for food, but if so, it was many centuries ago. There is no written history of that time."

Jean Marc asked, "What does your food taste like?"

"Taste?" Sacam had no answer for that. He slowly blinked his large eyes and said, "It is nourishment, I have never thought much about taste. It is an interesting concept. It's not unpleasant. It has small leaves and seeds and algae in it. I also have some that contain bits of what you might call dried fruits and nuts mixed in. That one tends to be popular with the children of my world for what you would call snacking. I do not care for the sweetness of it, so I carry this green one most often when I travel. He reached inside a pocket of his silver suit and pulled out a small shiny green square. He tore open the clear packet and pulled out a dense green cake and broke it in half and took a bite. He handed the other piece to Jean Marc. I think that it is safe for you to eat. Try it. Then you can tell me how it tastes."

Jean Marc sniffed at the small green piece of food. It didn't have much of an odor. Then he took a small bite. It was dry and crumbly at first, but then melted in his mouth. He said, "It tastes like spinach." He laughed. "I don't like spinach very much." He spit the green stuff into his handkerchief and stuck it into his back pocket.

Sacam said, "I suppose that it tastes...what you would

call green. It has a large amount of what your scientists would call chlorophyll...I would say...it simply tastes green." He smiled and showed his tiny white teeth. "I have taken samples of the green algae that covers great areas of water here to be analyzed and it appears to be related to the algae that grows on my planet. I am intrigued by that notion. It makes me wonder how the algae got here. We are hoping to be able to find a way to use this algae for food in the event that one of us gets stranded here for a long period of time. It could happen. Our small shuttles are quite durable, but this terrain is difficult. Sometimes I think a place is a good landing spot and it turns out to be water covered in floating plant life and not a good place at all. It can be quite dangerous if I make a mistake and crash."

CHAPTER THIRTY-FOUR

Jean Marc could not even imagine living on a plant-based diet. He liked corn and rice as much as anyone, but living on dried-up algae and chewed-up leaves didn't sit well in his mind. Meats and seafood were as much a part of his life as his breath or skin. Trapping, for him, was simply a way to make money, but again, it was a part of his life that he could not imagine living without for any long period of time. His doing without his own usual kinds of food and without his fishing and hunting during the years he was away in the war was a bad enough memory and one that he did not want to repeat. He had seriously missed his favorite foods. Life must be very bland on Sacam's planet. A world without spicy crawfish étouffée or chicken gumbo would be bland and strange indeed. Maybe one day he would have to introduce Sacam to some of his mama's cooking.

Jean Marc was as curious about the everyday life that Sacam and his people live on his own planet as Sacam was about life here on Earth. They each asked questions and enjoyed learning about each other's world.

Sacam told him, "My daily routine is not so different from many of the Earth beings I have observed. My wife is named Meera. She is also a scientist. Both of us are interested in plants and insects. I visit this world and collect the examples of plant and insect life that I find here. I take those samples home to Meera. She is doing a catalog of all the smaller life forms that we have found here. She makes photographs and writes descriptions and puts in as much information as I can give her about each life form. It will take many years to finish, because this world is so full of life. We hope to publish it one day as a reference book for those who are interested in the smaller life forms of this planet."

Jean Marc asked, "Are there so many of your people that care about us here on Earth? Do so many want to know about our bugs?"

"Ohhh yes," Sacam replied. "There are many on my world who would love to come here. Our world is smaller and our number of actual travelers is quite small because of the expense, but yes, there are many who are interested. I have shown some of the work to the Galactic Exploration Department and they are absolutely as amazed as Meera and I have been. They have approved my journeys here for several more of our years to come. It is very exciting for us.

"We are very much like you Earthlings in our curiosity and love of knowledge. Meera and I have a child, a son, named Abboth who appears to be interested in following in our careers. He is twenty of our years old which would make him about fifteen of your Earth years. He is presently attending a school for science and will be finished in about five more years. Then he will join us in our work. When he is home from school with us on Holidays, we already enjoy having him work with us. He is very intelligent and quite entertaining, but I do admit that I may be slightly biased in my opinion." Sacam crinkled up his eyes and chuckled a little, which made him seem even more human to Jean Marc. He scrunched up his large eyes and his small mouth widened into a grin.

He continued, "We live in houses and sleep and eat and attend social gatherings much the same as Earth beings. Tell me about the big celebration that your people had a few days back. What was the celebration about? It appeared to be a joining for a couple of young people. I enjoyed the music, though it is quite different from music on my world. Ours is more soothing in nature, and a lot of the Earth music seems to be quite lively and very loud. I did find it to be quite exciting."

Jean Marc then spent some time telling him all about the wedding. Sacam was very amused by the idea of Michel dancing with the broom but appeared to be a little embarrassed by the idea of the shivaree. He had asked about mating, but it was very strange to see his white face go green when he blushed from his shyness at the mention of mating rituals. Jean Marc did not even attempt to describe the sexual act itself. Sacam assured Jean Marc that mating on Earth sounded very much like mating on his world except that they would never speak of it openly like that. Such things are very private to his people.

Although Sacam's description of life on his planet did not seem very different from the lives of people here on Earth, it sounded more like a city dweller's life than Jean Marc's own adventure-filled days here in rural Louisiana.

Sacam told him, "Though Meera stays behind to process the specimens after each of my visits to Earth, on my trip this time, I finally had to tell her that she may come with me at some time in the future, because she is so curious to see the place that has produced the unusual specimens that I brought for her to study. Besides the catalog that we are putting together, we are writing a detailed report on the blue planet, Earth, and its high numbers of life forms and the varied plant life. We are very excited about the report and hope that our scientific leaders will recognize the effort that we put into the project and give us an award or even a medal. That would add to our credentials and would help our catalog to sell when it is published."

CHAPTER THIRTY-FIVE

Jean Marc was surprised both that the beings from Sacam's world wrote and sold books and that medals were given on other worlds to recognize service, just as here on Earth. He tried to explain his own medals and even offered to show them to him, but Sacam could not understand how or why one group of people would try to kill another. The whole idea of political differences was beyond his comprehending. He said that there had not been a war on his world for many centuries.

Jean Marc asked, "How do your people settle their differences? Don't they fight with each other over differences of opinion or things like land or when someone does something another person doesn't like?"

Sacam told him, "We have panels of judges that listen to both sides of an argument and then make an effort to bring the parties to a mutual agreement. The panels work hard to settle every dispute and the parties involved have to agree to live by the final ruling of the committee if no agreement can be reached."

Jean Marc asked, "What do you do with those people who commit crimes? Do you put them in prison the way we do here?"

Sacam shook his head and looked puzzled. "We have

no crimes or prisons. Why would anyone want to do something that would be against the rules or that might hurt another person?"

A world without prisons was impossible to imagine for Jean Marc. No crime? No prisons? No crooked politicians?

Sacam told him that he used a different name for this planet but when he said it in his mind, there was no way Jean Marc could wrap his tongue around the peculiar-feeling word. It sounded right inside his head but he could not say the word out loud at all. They shared a few laughs over his attempts. Communication inside his head was beginning to feel very natural.

One afternoon Jean Marc paddled his pirogue deep into the swamp and threw out a line to fish. He usually liked to use his casting net but this was one of those warm and lazy days with dappled sunlight that made pole fishing seem like the perfect thing to do. Sacam came to the cove and waved to him from the bank of the river. Jean Marc pulled in his line and picked him up in his pirogue. They had an interesting few minutes discussing the homebuilt boat and how it was made. Fascinated by the many uses of the wood, Sacam was excited by the sheer numbers of kinds of wood that could be found there. His home planet had no trees that grew to a usable size because the land was generally too rocky to support that kind of life.

Sacam also watched Jean Marc use the paddles to move the boat through the water. He even took a turn at trying to use the paddles himself, but almost fell into the water. They shared more laughter as Sacam admitted that it looked much easier than it was. Jean Marc told him that he had been paddling a pirogue since he was a young boy, but admitted that he had fallen in the water a few times himself as he was learning. He picked up the long pole that he used when the water was too shallow to paddle and stood in the boat to show how it was done. Poling a flat-bottom pirogue was the easiest way to get around in a place full of slow-moving shallow water. Sacam did not want to try that method himself, although he found it fascinating to watch.

There seemed to be many things to learn and share about each other's worlds. They spent numerous afternoons fishing and laughing and learning about the similarities and differences between them. On this day, Sacam even tried his hand at casting the line out in the water. There was a red and white wooden bobber attached to the line that floated for a while and then suddenly dipped under the surface and headed away from the boat. It got Sacam all excited. He caught a fish, but was very uncomfortable about the thought of killing it, so Jean Marc took the hook out of the fish's mouth and let it swim away and then began to help Sacam gather the plants that he wanted to collect. Jean Marc told him the names of the ones he knew and also gave him information about their medicinal as well as culinary uses. He offered the flavors of mint and cattail root. He gathered the wild grapes and mushrooms. Jean Marc tried to get him to taste the sweet grapes, but Sacam told him that he could not taste foods until tests were run to make sure that his system could tolerate them. What is good food to some could be dangerous to others. Jean Marc had never thought of it from that viewpoint. That explained why the man in the silver suit had not accepted his many offerings of food.

Sacam looked at the box full of specimens and smiled, "You Earth people have a world that is so diverse. My planet does not have one tenth of the living plants or animals that you have here. I am totally amazed by the new things I find with every visit. I have traveled to every corner of this planet and every place is different. The soil is different, the animals are different. There is water all over and most of it is clean and filled with living things. Another thing about this planet is that the beings who inhabit it are all so different in appearance. The people in each section of this world look and live differently from the others. Some of the beings have dark skin and some are light. Some have body parts and even facial features that seem to have evolved to suit the conditions of that place. Some are tall and some are much shorter. The Creator has been very generous to this world. Our planet is much smaller and my people basically all look similar. We have bred out all the differences over the centuries and now we are all homogenized into this one kind of being. We can tell each other apart but I doubt that many Earth people could tell which of us was which. We all speak the same language too. There was perhaps a time when our people had some differences but I can see now that those differences would have caused tension. I see the results of those tensions here on your world. Eventually the differences were all blended together by interbreeding. It is easier that way. Although we do not have the wars or the problems that your people seem to keep having, I have to admit that it is not nearly as interesting."

CHAPTER THIRTY-SIX

Jean Marc had heard Sacam mention the Creator several times and he finally got up enough nerve to ask. "Sacam, when you mention the Creator, do you mean that you worship God? Is it the same God that we worship here? We also call our God the Creator."

Sacam thought a minute before answering. "I do not know this being that you call God. We do not worship The Creator as much as we respect and honor Him but then I suppose that could be interpreted as a form of worship. He made the universe and all that is in it. I have noticed that you talk to your God. We do that with our Creator too. We thank him for his generosity and we do occasionally ask for guidance."

Jean Marc told him, "I have always been taught that God created the universe and everything in it, so God must be the same as the Creator that you and your people honor. Don't you think?"

Sacam agreed that it seemed logical to think that one God could have done it all. Jean Marc had a lot of questions about worship. He discovered that on Sacam's world there were no separate religions or churches. They had no priests or ministers, no statues or saints. The relationship between God and the beings was very personal and left to each individual to develop or not. Everyone followed the rules set up in the teachings of the Creator but it was not thought of as a religion as it is here on Earth. The teachings were available for all to read and although some have studied and make a living by teaching them, they were not treated differently because of that choice. They were teachers but not what Earthmen would call priests. They wielded no more power than a teacher of any other subject.

Sacam continued to explain, "Every person has something that interests them more than anything else, or a talent for something that makes them better at that one thing. The laws of nature allow the best to rise to the top naturally and the rest settle in where their skills or work ethic place them. There are those who work very hard to rise in their chosen field and then there are those who are content to do just enough to get by. They are free to make their own choices as long as those choices do not interfere with anyone else. When a conflict arises, a Committee of Elders is chosen to settle the differences."

Jean Marc thought it all sounded very civilized and peaceful. He especially liked the part about the Creator but was a little confused that there was no Church.

Both of them were surprised but also both took some comfort in knowing that even though they were from different worlds, God or the Creator was still watching over them both. Somehow the universe felt much smaller and more intimate for both of them when they thought about it that way.

The sun was going down very quickly and the stars reflected on the surface of the water, lighting the way back to Jean Marc's house on stilts. They enjoyed the silent companionship. It had been a very satisfying day. They had almost reached the curve where the big gator had lived for so many years and Jean Marc was glad that his new friend had survived the attack. Sacam was glad as well and said a silent "thank you" again in his mind as they headed for the spot.

Jean Marc lifted the pole to push again and heard the honking horn of Boo's old truck, the signal that Boo was looking for him. He sent a quick thought to Sacam to duck down in the boat so that his friends would not see him. Then he pushed the boat over to the bank and quickly offloaded the boxes of plants and seeds and roly-poly bugs that they had collected that day. They moved quickly and hoped that Boo and Elloi did not come crashing through the woods to catch them in the act. He was certainly not ashamed of his new friend. He would have loved to introduce them to each other and give them all a chance to learn from each other, but he was concerned for Sacam's safety. Boo would probably be pleased to know Sacam and could most likely be trusted with the secret, but Elloi was a little loose in the lips sometimes and was not as good at keeping secrets…especially if he had been drinking beer.

As soon as the boxes were onshore, Sacam jumped out and waved goodbye to his earthly friend and Jean Marc pushed off into the current and let out a yell to tell Boo and Elloi that he was on his way back home.

CHAPTER THIRTY-SEVEN

Boo and Elloi were parked in front of Jean Marc's house. They wanted him to go to the tavern down the road and shoot some pool, and Elloi hoped to find some ladies who were willing to dance and make a little romance. Elloi Comeaux was a big guy, but he loved to dance and he loved the ladies. Jean Marc was a little uncertain about dancing the night away with his leg still hurting sometimes, but he decided to go along and sit and drink a few beers if nothing else. He had slow-danced a little at Marguerite's wedding a while back but did not feel ready to tackle a full evening of lively dancing to the Cajun music that he loved. Still, he would enjoy an evening of fun and listening to the music.

The possibility of meeting a lady was intriguing. Maybe it was time now that he stopped nursing his broken heart and looked around for someone else to soothe his troubled spirit. He tied up the boat and let out a yell as he decided that tonight was going to be a night of fun. Why not? He was unattached and there might be someone special out there waiting for him to make a move.

After washing up quickly and changing into a clean shirt and pants, he climbed into the truck with his friends. They roared off down the dirt road with the dust flying out behind them. Boo was singing his funny song:

Elloi Comeaux gonna dance the night away
even if he's gotta dance all by hisself.
Elloi gotta find a lady, yeah, yeah yeah.

It made them all laugh and set the mood for the evening.

Jean Marc had watched for Sacam as they pulled out onto the gravel road, but only saw the flash of silver shooting across the sky. He wondered if that meant that he had taken the specimens they collected back for his wife to process. He wondered about a trip to travel the many thousands of miles in the space between this planet and Sacam's home and decided that it would be the most interesting thing he could imagine. He wanted to see Earth from way out there and he wanted to find out more about the kind of engine that could make the journey without any sound.

He liked the idea of his new friend having a family. Everyone should have a family. One day maybe he would have a family of his own. He had to have faith.

Boo pulled the old truck into the open spot in front of the bar. The music was loud and the ladies were in a friendly mood in the Corner Pocket Café and Bar tonight— he could tell by the shadows of couples hiding at the corners of the building and under the big oak tree. Jean Marc decided to put away just enough beer to dull both the ache in his leg and the ache in his heart. When the three of them swept through the door Elloi quickly grabbed a pretty girl and found a place in the moving circle of dancers. Jean Marc was a little bit slower but after a few minutes, he sang along with the band and danced a little. He let the smiling eyes of his partner hypnotize him into forgetting about the loss of his lovely Amy. She smiled and his spirits lifted immediately.

The pretty girl was not his love, but she was warm and laughing and let him hold her hand for a moment even after the music stopped. She looked familiar to him. He felt a kind of closeness almost as if they had known each other for a long time but he could not put his finger on where he may have met her before; however, Butte La Rose was a small community surrounded by more small communities and he had most likely met almost everyone within a fifty-mile radius at one time or another during his lifetime.

When his leg began to hurt, he explained that he needed to rest for a bit and she seemed to understand. They went to a quiet corner table in the back of the place and sat together and talked and smoked cigarettes and she even let him hold her fingertips as they talked and he was encouraged by that. He wanted to feel accepted again. Amy's betrayal had damaged his self-confidence to the point that it would have been difficult for him to speak to this girl had it not been for the enthusiasm of his friends. He had nodded his head to her and smiled his crooked smile, but was then overcome by a strange shyness. His pulse began racing and his tongue felt thick. Fortunately, Frank Soilleau, the bartender, had introduced them as Jean Marc stood near her at the bar when he went to order a beer. She told him that her name was Emmaline but he could call her Emma. It was a nice name. It felt soft and warm in his mind and tasted good in his mouth and rolled off the tongue with ease. After a few moments' time, his heart settled down and they got along well and made easy conversation. They seemed to laugh at the same things and both seemed to find excuses to lightly touch fingers as often as they could. Jean Marc was feeling better than he had in years.

CHAPTER THIRTY-EIGHT

Over by the pool tables across the room, there was a ruckus going on. Several of the local bad boys were there drinking too much and trying to start a fight strictly for the purpose of entertainment. So far, no one had taken them up on the idea.

Jean Marc stood up to make sure that Boo and Elloi were not involved and then sat back down to continue his flirting with Emma. The more they talked, the more he decided that he liked her. She had a pretty smile and her eyes were as blue as a summer sky. She made him laugh and he soon realized that he was having a very good time. It was the second very good time he had enjoyed since he got home. The first was the time spent on the gator hunt the night that Boo's son was born. Maybe normal did still exist, after all. Then he realized that he had also very much enjoyed his day with Sacam, but was not ready to call that "normal" quite yet.

Jean Marc and Emma both jumped back quickly when the back half of a broken pool-cue landed on the table in front of them with a loud cracking noise. Jean Marc stood up quickly and stepped in front of the girl to protect her from whatever else might come flying in their direction. The largest and drunkest of the bad boys stomped over to retrieve his weapon, but Jean Marc picked it up first and held it out in front of himself between his two hands to protect himself and Emma. One of the others in the man's group yelled out in a mocking sing-song voice, "Git him, Andre, das our local War Hero."

The one they called Andre hissed at him, "Is dat true, yeah? You dat Army man? Show us your medals, Mister Army man, Mr. War Hero!...or better yet, show us what you got!" He pulled back his fist to hit Jean Marc in the face.

Jean Marc had certainly never intended to get into a fight tonight. He had never enjoyed fighting; his brother, Aaron, had always been known as the fighter in the family. But he felt obligated to protect this girl and besides, he was not going to back down and look cowardly in front of his friends. He might not like fighting but he was more than capable if he had to. Uncle Sam had taught him well. Jean Marc dodged one meaty fist and landed a punch on the side of the big guy's jaw.

Jean Marc reached out and grabbed Andre's wrist in his own strong hand and twisted it around behind the man's back, pulled it up high and said into his ear, "Yeah, I was a soldier and I damned sure ain't ashamed of it and yeah, I got me some medals in the war...and yeah buddy, I can whoop your ass if you want me to. But I think that you and your rowdy friends ought to quit your little banty rooster games and call it a night."

He looked over to see that Boo had one of the others hemmed up against the pool table and Elloi had the third one face down on the ground with a boot on the back of his neck. There was a little bit of a huff and scuffle and a few colorful words when Jean Marc turned his guy loose but all in all it ended well and the trio left the bar. The lead singer in the band stepped up to the microphone and said, "Ahhh…yeahhhhh…how 'bout we have us a little two-step like they do next door in Texas?" The music started up again and everybody breathed a little easier after that.

Jean Marc turned his attention back to Emma. He told her, "I'm sorry about this, Emmaline; I didn't mean to get you involved in a fight."

"I know. It wasn't your fault." She calmly took a clean handkerchief from her pocket and wiped at his chin but was glad to see the spot of blood that she wiped away did not belong to him.

The waitress brought them each a beer and told them that Mr. Giraud, the owner, said that it was on the house and thanks for clearing out the riff-raff. Them *coullions* have been trying to get something going ever since they came in the place. Jean Marc said his thanks and took a sip. It was the good stuff. He nodded and grinned at Emma.

Boo and Elloi came to drag him away a little after eleven. Boo said that he was trying to be good to Marie since she blessed him with his son. When that didn't work , he finally admitted that she had told him that she would get out her trusty rolling pin if he didn't come home early and he was already late. Elloi was about ready to pass out from all the alcohol he had consumed. Boo threatened to toss him in the bed of the truck if he threw up.

Jean Marc stood up to leave but it was clear that Emma had other ideas. She held onto his hand and said that if he would stay there with her a little while longer, she would see that he got home later. So he sent his friends on their way with them both smirking at him and he stayed a while longer to spend more time with Emma.

There was something special about the girl that made him feel hope for the future again. He dared to believe in that feeling. Another good point in her favor was that she had her own pickup truck and knew how to drive it. They talked and danced and held hands until the bartender told them he was closing the place down and they had to leave.

Jean Marc had not ever before felt this comfortable with a girl in his entire life, not even with Amy, which came as a surprise when he thought about it. Emma seemed to be interested in his thoughts and opinions about everything and yet she offered her own thoughts and opinions in a quiet and gentle way without being argumentative even when they disagreed. They had fun and seemed to know the same people.

Jean Marc listened to the music and felt the buzz from the beer and thought that he was tired but very happy. It had been a good day and a better evening.

How could I not know this girl? I had to have met her. Why can't I remember? Had I been so blinded by Amy that I didn't even see other women? he thought. It was true that he had pretty much kept his mind on Amy, although there was a brief relationship with a nurse in the last hospital. He had felt guilty about it but after a few weeks, the nurse was transferred to another location and she had been the one to break it off, so he didn't feel so bad after that.

He sat back in his chair and looked at Emma. She

leaned back in her own chair and looked right back at him and laughed. He was intrigued.

When he had tried to talk to Amy about anything, it was always an effort to hold her interest unless the topic of discussion was Amy herself or something that she was interested in. Jean Marc finally had to admit that Amy had usually done most of the talking when they were together. He could never remember her asking him for his opinion on anything and when he volunteered an opinion, she usually ignored it or said that she was not sure about that and would have to ask her papa. He could remember wondering several times if she was planning to ask her papa about all of the questions that would come up in their lives. It had annoyed him, but he had put those feelings aside. She had agreed to become his wife and he would have liked to feel that she would have confidence in his thoughts and his way of doing things. Looking back, he began to see that perhaps he had been blinded by his infatuation and his life with Amy may not have been as perfect as he once believed. Maybe his mama had been right.

This girl was very different from the other girls that he had been around. They both had the feeling that this meeting was the beginning of something special. She had not been drinking as much beer as he had, so she drove him home in her truck. It was a short trip, but they laughed all the way there. He thought about kissing her goodnight but chickened out. He was afraid that she would think he was being too pushy, so he opened the door and started to get down. She grabbed him by the arm and leaned over and softly kissed him on the lips before he climbed out of the cab of the truck. It wasn't a big kiss, but it was nice. She had a sweet smile on her face and Jean Marc wore a silly grin as he closed the door of the truck. He had never had a woman lead the way like that in the kissing department and he kind of liked it. She wasn't aggressive about it. She seemed to know somehow that he was too shy to initiate the kiss himself, no matter how badly he wanted to. She managed to do the deed without making him feel at all diminished. He felt flattered and happy. He whistled a silly tune as he climbed the steps to his own front porch and watched her drive away back down the road. Tonight had been fun. He hoped to see Emma again very soon.

Chili came running around the corner of the house to see what he was whistling about. Then Jean Marc realized that he had forgotten to get her last name and he didn't even know where she lived. He felt like an idiot. Here was the first woman he'd met in years that made him feel something other than simple lust, and even though they had talked for hours and talked about all the friends and relatives they both knew, he didn't even ask her name. He confessed his stupid mistake to Chili, but the dog offered him no comfort. The dog looked at him like he agreed that it was indeed a pretty stupid thing to do.

CHAPTER THIRTY-NINE

The next day he did his work as quickly as he could manage. For the first time, he was grateful that the catch was smaller than usual. As soon as the work was done, Jean Marc got bathed and dressed in record time. He hurried back toward the bar to see if she was there or if somebody knew her. Joe the bartender had introduced them so he was hoping to find out more from him, if he was on duty tonight.

He found her sitting outside on the wooden steps of the tavern porch wearing a sleeveless summer dress and open-toed sandals and looking beautiful. Her long blonde hair was loose and free and moving gently in the breeze. She smiled at him as though she knew all along that he would be coming back. He sat down on the steps beside her and they smoked cigarettes and talked some more. They never seemed to run out of things to talk about. It wasn't all one-sided either. Once again, they shared the conversation and exchanged ideas and even disagreed on a few things in a playful manner that did not seem uncomfortable at all. They finally went inside for a bowl of gumbo and a beer and to dance, but by the time they got on the dance floor they both realized that dancing was not what either of them had in mind.

Emma had never felt this kind of immediate connection with a man before but she believed in the feeling and trusted her heart. Her heart told her that in spite of the short time she had known this particular man, he was the one. She decided then and there to have faith in him and in herself. It was an easy decision even though she had never felt this way before; somehow, she was not afraid. It felt right. They walked around to the back of the building in a darker area under the trees and kissed and talked until things were beginning to get out of control, and then Jean Marc told her that he needed to walk a bit. She understood and agreed to meet him the next evening. They both had a lot of thinking to do.

Over the next couple of weeks, time dragged on forever when they were apart but flew by when they were together. The chores took more effort than usual and Jean Marc finally admitted that he didn't want to be doing chores; he wanted to be with Emma. He did his work anyway, but may have taken more shortcuts than he should have taken. He did not see Sacam at all for a few days and wondered if he was still at his own home and hoped that he was safe and had not had any more run-ins with alligators. One evening, he walked to the tavern and stood leaning against the porch railing until he saw Emma's truck. When she climbed down from the driver's side door he met her there and kissed her hello. He could tell from her response that this night was going to be different. Her kisses were eager and she looked into his eyes after each one as though looking for some kind of confirmation. The time was right to take their relationship to the next level. He wanted her. She evidently wanted him too. Nature was pushing them toward that step without regard for the rules or the lessons they had both had drilled into their heads throughout their upbringing by their parents and Church.

He whispered, "Let's walk to my house."

She gave him a shy smile and whispered back, "We can take my truck."

He said, "No. I think I would rather walk."

"Why?" she asked.

"I don't know...just feels right somehow."

They began to walk down the road for the mile or so to his house. After a few minutes, Jean Marc dropped behind a step or two and watched her walking ahead of him while he took great pains to light his cigarette. Her trim figure swayed...no, that's not right, he thought, she "sashayed" as she put one foot in front of the other. He liked it.

She stopped, turned around and propped one hand on her waist, and asked, "What are you doing back there?"

He looked at her with that sheepish little boy smile and told her the truth, "I was watching your behind as you walked. It kind of sways back and forth...sashays... I read that word someplace...I like it." He grinned as he said it. "Emmaline sashays when she walks down the road." He laughed and imitated the way she walked beside her, swaying his hips in an effeminate way.

She playfully hit his arm and said, "Jean Marc Thibodaux, that is so bad! I can't believe I was even considering letting you kiss me again." But she didn't look at all upset. She was grinning back at him.

He said, "No...that is not bad, it is being honest...I wanted to see your behind when you walked...so I looked."

He tossed the cigarette into the ditch that ran beside the road and took her face in his two hands and kissed her right there in front of God and everybody. It was so sweet and tender that it nearly made his heart stop.

She held on to fistfuls of his shirt front and stood on her tip-toes, looked him in the eye for a few seconds, and then said, "Well?"

"Well, what?" he asked.

She stomped her foot impatiently on the gravel road and said, "Well, if you are going to stop in the middle of the road to look at my behind, was it worth it?"

He started walking again and chuckled as he told her, "I wasn't the one who stopped. I only slowed down a little bit."

She hit him on the arm again and walked beside him but she was grinning. Jean Marc rubbed his arm.

"Girl, you gotta stop hitting on me. I'm gonna be black and blue if you keep doin' that, yeah. Didn't your mama teach you not to hit guys? Some of them might hit back."

He could see her face in the moonlight. She was very pretty when she was pretending to be angry. He liked that. He wanted to kiss her again right there in the middle of the road, but was afraid that if he did it, he would not be able to stop with kisses. With his luck somebody would run over them both laying there in the road all naked and sweaty. Then he would have to listen to Boo and Elloi pick at him about it for the rest of his natural life. He could wait. They were not too far from his house. Once they got there, he planned to kiss her. He planned to kiss her a lot. Again he had to compare this feeling of need and overwhelming desire to the years he spent with Amy. There had been times when he had wanted to love her but had never lost control. He had told himself that it was because he wanted to do what was right. Now he knew that the real reason was that he had not felt the deep burning passion for Amy that he was feeling for Emma. He and Emma were truly meant to be together. Jean Marc believed that with all his heart. This was the woman he wanted to marry and make babies with and grow old with. His mama had been right. This was the woman that had been waiting for him.

When they got to the house, Chili came running up to get his usual attention and was properly introduced to Miss Emmaline Hebert. He even raised his paw to shake hands with her. She was thrilled. Chili seemed impressed with her too. He ran around them both and put his knobby old head into both their hands for petting. Jean Marc took that as approval, but left him outside on the porch all the same. Chili lay down on the braided rag rug in front of the closed front door and seemed content.

Jean Marc went very slowly with her. He made a pot of coffee in the tall drip coffeepot and he kissed her gently and asked, "Emma, do you know why we are here? Are you sure that you want to stay with me tonight?"

She looked him square in the eye and said, "Yes."

She softly said, "Jean Marc, I am twenty-two years old, not some seventeen-year-old girl. I've already made the decision in my mind and I know that I am ready to be with you. I think that we are always going to be together. Does that thought scare you? I want to be here but I want to because I want to belong to you. I love you."

He said, "Yeah, I do too, I mean…no, it doesn't scare me at all. I like that idea a lot. And I think I love you too. But Emma, do you know what you are letting yourself in for? Have you ever been with a man before? I'm not judging, I just want to know. I don't want to scare you or hurt you in any way."

Blushing from the top of her head to her knees, she said, "No, I don't know what to expect, not exactly, I have never been with a man, but I have talked to my married friends and I kind of know some of it and…I know that I trust you and I am ready to go on with it anyway." Her face was red as a beet but she did not look afraid.

He kissed her softly and then held her close. She buried her face in his shirt and tried to forget that part of their conversation.

Jean Marc had been pleased to find out that he was to be her first lover. He had also been very flattered. It made him feel even more certain that this relationship was meant to be. To know that Emma had given serious thought to her decision and still had chosen to stay was a very important point.

He was very respectful and gentle with her. He tried to imagine that she was already his wife and he treated her the way he would have if this were their wedding night. In his mind, it was a wedding night in God's eyes. He wanted her to enjoy the experience but he also wanted her to know that she was loved. They spent the rest of that night talking and touching and making love and then sleeping until the sun was well up in the sky.

Jean Marc gently removed himself from the bed to make a pot of coffee and to say good morning to the world. He also relieved his bladder off the side of the back porch the way he had done for most of his life. Emma made him breakfast when she got up a few minutes later. She scrambled some eggs and toasted a couple of yesterday's biscuits in the skillet to eat with them. Jean Marc opened a jar of his mama's home-made pear preserves to add to the meal, even though he personally thought the kisses he got between bites were plenty sweet enough for him. They sat together at the little table and held hands as they drank their coffee. Jean Marc smiled an honest, happy smile for the first time in a very long time. When she stood up to take the dishes to the dishpan, he asked if she were still willing to keep seeing him from now on and she shyly nodded her head and answered that she would like that very much. He was glad and told her so. The whole scene felt normal and domestic and he could very easily imagine his life going on like this for many years to come. It was a very good feeling.

CHAPTER FORTY

She was beautiful. She stood there smiling at him, wearing nothing but her cotton panties and his old work shirt, looking prettier than the posters of the Hollywood pin-up girls that his buddies used to collect in the Army. Both of them openly admitted now that their situation was strange and wonderful. Both liked that their being together felt so natural. They were both relaxed and content.

He asked, "How long you been living here in Butte La Rose?"

Emma told him, "I came to stay almost a year ago from Baton Rouge to take care of my sick grandmother and I did that until Grandmère passed a few months ago. She left me her house and now I have been trying to decide if I should go back to Baton Rouge or stay here and live in that house. You know the house up past the store that has the big side porch and the green front door? I have been wrestling with the decision for several months and a few weeks ago, I finally decided to go back home to Baton Rouge. I went to the bar that night we met as a goodbye treat to myself before leaving. They do make a good gumbo and I had packed up my stuff to leave and didn't want to mess up the kitchen that night. Now," she said as she ran her fingers through her long blonde hair, "you, Mr. Thibodaux, are making me rethink that idea of going back home to Baton Rouge. I unpacked my stuff."

And Jean Marc smiled while looking into her smiling blue eyes and said, "I'm glad. I don't want you to leave."

He kissed her softly and led her back to the wrinkled bed and did his very best to show her more reasons for not going away.

During the afterglow, he asked, "What was your grand-mère's name, *Sha*? I knew the lady that lived in that house."

She responded, "Grandmère's name was Antoinette Leleux Hebert."

He was shocked. He said, "Well, yeah, wasn't she called Tante Nettie?"

She sat up on one elbow and said, "Yes, she was called Tante Nettie by everybody but me. She was always just Grandmère to me."

He sat up and bunched his pillow up behind him so that he was propped in a sitting position. "Oh Lord, *Sha*, I have known Tante Nettie for most all my life...I was away in the war when she passed or I would have been at her funeral. Mama wrote to me about her passing. She said Tante Nettie had been bad sick for a long time. She was our *treateur* and my mama's close friend. I remember the first time Mama and Papa brought me in a wagon to visit her for a terrible earache when I was a real little boy. Tante Nettie said prayers for me and she blew cigarette smoke into my ear with a rolled-up piece of brown paper bag. I can still remember that it hurt like a sumbitch and I was crying because I was scared. I was kicking and screaming like crazy. It took all of the grown-ups to hold me down to do it. But my ear got better. She took care of all of my family when they got sick. In fact, most everybody who lives here has probably been treated by Tante Nettie over the years. She was well known and well loved and respected too. Did you ever visit her here?"

"Yep, sure did... from the time I was about five years old until I was about fourteen or so, I spent every summer here after school was out. We were very close. I loved being with her. Grandmère helped so many people, but the one that she was not able to help was herself. She caught what she called a cancer of the blood and by the end, she grew so weak that she could barely sit up in her chair. She was so tiny and frail that even I could pick her up and carry her in my arms like a small child. It was very hard seeing her help so many others with their illnesses and not be able to help her own. But there is no cure for what she had."

He said, "Tante Nettie was a good woman who lived her whole life to help others. I remember Mama going to visit her lots of times, because they were friends. I used to tag along with her sometimes on Sundays and there was a little girl there that I used to play with. She had long blonde braids...did you know her? I can't remember her name, but I remember that we used to have fun. We would play *treateur* to her doll. We would mix up all kinds of stuff to treat the dolly's made-up illnesses. I had no idea what I was doing, but it didn't seem to matter. I liked that little girl. But I don't know what happened to her. I guess we got older and I moved in with my papaw to help him when he got older. Then after he passed, I went into the Army."

Emma looked at him with wide eyes. "That was me, Jean Marc. I was the only one that ever came to stay with her. I had long braids. It had to be me. Can you believe it? We played together when we were little. Isn't that strange? I have felt like I knew you from the first time we saw each other that night at the bar. I just couldn't figure out how."

CHAPTER FORTY-ONE

She was afraid to put her real thoughts into words, but could not help thinking that perhaps her secret prayers were being answered. She remembered the boy she used to play with as a child and had often wondered where he had gone and if he grew up to be handsome. She had daydreamed about him for years. Now she knew that he was not only handsome, he was a good man and she wanted to think that a future was possible for them as a couple.

Figuring out that they had played together during his family visits to the *treateur's* house was exciting for them both. They looked closely at each other's faces, trying to remember how they had looked back then. It did help to explain the instant familiarity they both felt when they met. They had known each other off and on from the time they were small children until they were in their early teen years. But they had not seen each other for a long time. Grandmère and Grandpapa had gone to stay with Emma's family in Baton Rouge for a year or so while her Grandpapa was ill and Grandmère stayed a while longer after he passed on. Grandmère brought Emma with her when she came back home and they stayed here during the war and then she got sick and passed on while Jean Marc was away.

They laughed as they recalled the mischief they had

gotten into when they were small. Emma asked, "Do you remember that time we had been trying to draw some water from the well to give to my little dog? We somehow managed to drop the bucket down inside the well and lost the end of the rope. You remember?"

Jean Marc said, "I remember it all right. I fell in the well when I stood on the side and tried to grab the rope to get the bucket out. You ran to get help and your papa and mine came running outside with another long rope. Thank the blessed Saviour, I had found a piece of rock sticking out and managed to stand on that little sliver of rock until the line got to me. I wrapped the rope around my hand and hung on and somehow they pulled and I climbed up the sides of the well and into my papa's arms. He hugged me so tight I couldn't breathe and then he whipped my butt so hard I was not sure that I was gonna be able to sit down. Your papa asked me why I didn't get the bucket, while I was down there, and all of the adults laughed, like that was a good joke. I was so embarrassed. I remember rubbing my sore behind and saying that I might have been better off if I had stayed down there. They all laughed at that too and then Papa gathered me up in his arms and hugged me again.

"Papa kept saying, 'Thank you, Jesus, Thank you Jesus.' I remember thinking that my papa was the one who threw me the rope. But I was not about to say it out loud, cause I would have gotten another whoopin' for sure." They both laughed out loud.

Jean Marc looked deeply into her eyes and said, "See there, girl, you've been getting me into trouble ever since we were little kids and look at us now...you gonna get me into trouble some more, aren't you?"

She placed both hands on his face and kissed him softly. He groaned and said, "Ooooh yeahhh, I feel trouble brewing, all right. You are gonna bring me lots of trouble. I can tell."

But they held each other tightly and both of them were smiling.

CHAPTER FORTY-TWO

Emma's parents still lived in Baton Rouge. Her grandmère had very much wanted her to move here to Butte la Rose permanently and learn to be a *treateur* herself. Emma had considered doing exactly that because Grandmère had said many times that she had the gift, but it would be up to her own heart and mind to decide if she had the calling.

All during Emma's life, Grandmère had taught her about the treatments for each ailment and the herbs and recipes for the powders and elixirs to ease the pain and suffering she saw around her. Emma had always soaked up the lessons like a sponge. She learned how to pray for God's will to be done and how to ask for the healing blessings and powers to be sent to help that person recover. They spent hours out in the swampy woods collecting herbs and then tying them into bundles to hang up to dry or steeping them in water or alcohol to make the various tinctures or elixirs. Over the years, Emma had written it all down in lined notebooks like the ones she used in school. Grandmère had tested her many times by asking questions and was thrilled to see that Emma almost inevitably answered correctly, even when she was a very young girl. It seemed that she was gifted. Not only was she good at remembering the healing treatments but she also had a healing touch. There had been many times when Grandmère would have her help with a treatment by also laying her own small hands on the patient and even saying the special prayers in her young girl's voice. The people readily accepted her touch and felt certain that she would grow up to be as good as her grandmother at channeling God's healing strength to the sick and the weary. The people felt it was natural for her to be there at her grandmother's side and had no problem with it at all. No one had ever objected to her helping in their treatment. Emma loved working beside her grandmother. She got a kind of personal satisfaction from helping others that she never felt from anything else in her life.

When she gave a treatment to someone, Grandmère would never ask for money for payment, but if given a chicken or a small amount of money freely without having asked for it, then she would accept it and that is how she had lived. She would not ever be rich because her patients were not rich, but she got by pretty well and was never hungry. There were always lots of eggs and chickens and butter and even some piglets and lambs. She would find baskets of corn or tomatoes or other vegetables on the front steps almost every day during the growing season and someone was regularly dropping off extras after a fishing trip. She and Grandmère put up the fruit and vegetables in glass jars and stored them to use during the winter months. They stored the meats and some fish in the smokehouse and never went hungry.

Jean Marc seriously hoped that Emma would stay and practice her craft here in Butte La Rose. There was a real

medical doctor in Lafayette now and also one in Baton
Rouge, but that was a long ride away if a person was sick or
injured or only feeling down, and a *treateur* was very much
respected and considered to be a necessity in these rural
areas. Baton Rouge was growing into a large city. Out here
in the basin, a *treateur* was a blessing. As far as Jean Marc
knew, without Tante Nettie, there was no one here to heal
the people.

Emma said, "I came to be with Grandmère and to settle
things after she passed on. The only reason that I decided
to go home was that I have been so lonely here. I was not
sure that I was good enough to be a *treateur* without Grandmère's help. She was always there to ask if I had a question."

Jean Marc responded, "*Sha*, you don't have to be lonely
anymore because now you have me. As soon as people
realize that you are taking your grandmère's place as *treateur*, then you will be too busy to feel lonely. Everyone here
loved Tante Nettie and there will be plenty for you to do. If
we tell them that you are here, they will come. You got all
that stuff she taught you written down in those notebooks.
So you can look it up if you have a question, don't you
think? You only need to have a little faith in yourself and
in what you know in your heart. Nobody expects you to be
perfect. They just need somebody to try and help if they
can. You can do that, I know. I am surprised that they are
not keeping you busy now. Do they know you are here?"

She said, "I have kept to myself a lot. There was so
much to think about and such big decisions to make. I have
not been out to be with people, and I suspect most of the
locals thought I had gone back home to Baton Rouge. I

debated about going to Marguerite's wedding a few months back but I didn't go. I was feeling pretty sorry for myself about that time and just wanted to go home.

Jean Marc told her, "Well, that is about to change, my baby, you had better make sure you have plenty of all those medicines mixed up, because you are about to get real busy. You may wish for peace and quiet before it is over." He laughed and they got up and bathed and dressed. They both felt stronger and ready to face the world together as a couple.

CHAPTER FORTY-THREE

The very next night, Jean Marc took Emma to visit his family for dinner. He knew that Mama would not mind putting an extra plate at the table and he was also sure that she would be very glad to see the granddaughter of her old friend. He was right, of course. When they arrived, Jean Marc led Emma up the steps and into the kitchen. He went in the door yelling loudly to his mother that he brought an extra mouth to feed. She was juggling pots on the stovetop and yelled back that it was no problem, that there was plenty of food. Then she turned around and saw the guest. She squealed and hugged Emmaline like a long lost relative. Mama said that she had heard that Emma had gone back to Baton Rouge with her family. They spent almost the whole evening talking about Emma's grandmère and about Emma's taking over her practice.

Mama said, "Oh, *Sha*, I will gladly pass the word to all Tante Nettie's friends here and before long there will be sick people coming from all over the basin to be cured. They are your friends too. You know a lot of them and the rest will get to know you quick."

She said, "In fact, I need a treatment now for my rheumatism. My old knees are killin' me. It happens every year about this time."

Emma told her, "I will make you a bottle of willow bark elixir to take for it and bring it to you tomorrow. That will help with the redness and the swelling and make it feel a lot better."

His mother was pleased. She thought to herself, *Life definitely has its twists and turns. One moment, Jean Marc was lonely and feeling so down that he could not see that he even had a future. The next moment, he was reunited with this lovely girl that he had played with countless times growing up and from the looks of things, he was feeling the pain of loneliness going completely away.* She was very pleased. Emma was a nice girl from a good family and she was already someone that she could easily love as a daughter. She dared to hope that this girl would heal her son and make a good wife for him. She even hoped that they didn't wait too long to make the big announcement.

On the walk back to drop Emma off at her house, she and Jean Marc stood on the riverbank and watched the nighttime show of stars and lightning bugs, and both of them decided that life was not nearly so bad as it had seemed a few short weeks ago. A silver streak of light shot across the sky and headed down toward earth. Jean Marc wondered if it was Sacam returning in his silver air machine. He secretly hoped that it was. He had a thing or two to show him in the swamp and a personal thing or two to tell him as well.

Emma pointed to the sky and squealed, "Look, a shooting star! Let's make a wish." They held hands and each closed their eyes and made their silent wishes, but Jean Marc was thinking that even though Sacam's aircraft hardly qualified for a wishing star, his own wish was already coming true and so it didn't matter. He simply smiled and kissed Emma on the forehead.

"How will we know if we did it right?" he asked.

"If the wishes come true then I guess we did," she laughed.

CHAPTER
FORTY-FOUR

The next evening, Emma had gone back to Baton Rouge to get some more of her personal items from her parents' house. To Jean Marc, that showed that she was staying in town and so he was glad, even if it did mean missing one night of her company. Somehow it was still OK. He had faith in the relationship and was not too concerned.

Jean Marc arrived at his parents' house for dinner with a smile still plastered on his face and with Chili in his regular place in the bottom of the pirogue. After tying up to the shaky old dock in his usual place, he leapt out onto the rough-cut cypress boards with his mind full of Emmaline Hebert and the prospects of filling his belly with plenty of Mama's good cooking. For him, that was a promise of a pretty good evening. And it was also the night they usually listened to *Cousin Dud and the Hadacol Hour.*

He looked back at the dog, who was still stretched out in the bottom of the boat, and said, "You comin'? It's OK wit me if you want to keep layin' there. I'll just eat your share of supper." Chili lowered his head and laid it on his paws and made no effort to move. Jean Marc shook his head and laughed, "OK Chili-dog...suit yourself."

His long legs made strides along the worn path toward

the porch alone, but he stopped short when he recognized the voices coming from the front room.

Amy was talking fast and loud, like she was especially nervous, "We just felt that it was the right thing to do. And we just wanted to see this thing over and done. We don't want your family and ours to be keeping away from each other and having bad feelings for the rest of our lives, you know? So, we dropped by to say hello and to welcome Jean Marc back home, that's all."

She turned toward the open doorway when she heard Jean Marc's footsteps on the porch and they stood there looking at each other for what felt like a very long moment. It was one of those "time stood still" things that happen sometimes. Pierre got up from his ladder-backed chair and crossed the room to hold out his right hand in a cautious greeting. Jacque and Laurine, Jean Marc's parents, were each holding their breath and waiting to see how their son would react to seeing these two. These were the same two who had betrayed his trust while he was away in the war. None of them knew what to expect. The tension was so thick in the air that it crackled like tiny lightning bolts.

Jacque was seriously afraid that a fight would break out and the truth was that he could not blame his son if he did hit the guy. He would have already hit him if it had been him, that's for sure.

Jean Marc nodded solemnly and shook his old friend's hand and then nodded to Amy. Pierre let out a sigh of relief that echoed around the room and began to chatter nervously.

"How you doin', Jean Marc? Me and Amy just wanted

to drop by and tell you how glad we are that you made it home OK and we wanted to tell you that we're sorry about the way things happened between me and her and that we didn't mean to do nothing wrong," he said. "I was just tryin' to watch out for her like you axed me to do, you know"? He reached out to take his wife's hand and continued, "I love her, Jean Marc, I just couldn't help myself. I ain't sorry for that. But I am sorry that it hurt you. That's the truth. I don't know nothing more to say." He hung his head and looked at his feet.

Amy was twisting her dainty white handkerchief into a knot and her big brown eyes were brimming with tears as she stood there obviously pregnant and emotionally overwrought. She looked up at him with fear and self-recrimination in her eyes. She muttered, "I'm sorry too, Jean Marc, I'm so sorry. I was not trying to hurt you none. I just learned to love him and I just couldn't help it."

Jean Marc tried to summon up the old feelings, but all he felt was a kind of empty sadness. It was totally different from what he had expected to feel. He knew that it took a boat load of courage for these two to have come here this evening. He respected the fact that they wanted to clear the air this way. They were right. It was time to get it out in the open and deal with it. It would only get worse if they had let it fester over time.

Jean Marc felt a bit overwrought himself. He had imagined a hundred different scenes about seeing and talking to Amy again and had scripted the words that each of them would say in every circumstance…except this one. Somehow he had always managed to leave Pierre completely out of his daydreams. Now, they're all standing here together and Chili's idea of staying in the boat might have been a good idea after all. He could learn a lot if he paid more attention to that old dog. Chile was smarter than most humans that he knew.

He cleared his throat, focusing on the rough-cut cypress boards of the porch to give himself an extra minute of thinking time, and then looked at each of them in turn. "Look, it's done. OK, it's over. Y'all are married and you have a baby on the way. We all got to get on with livin' the way it is and not the way we might have wanted it to be one time. I'm doin' OK. It is what it is and that's all right. We are all gonna be perfectly fine. I know that y'all didn't mean to hurt anyone. So don't worry about it anymore, OK?"

Amy was crying openly now and Pierre moved over beside her to wrap one arm around her shoulders. He made soothing sounds to his wife and told Jean Marc, "We didn't go to do nothing wrong, Jean Marc. You just gotta know that."

"I do know that, Pierre. I was gone and you were both here together and y'all were able to see each other all the time and that was the way it was, that's all. I'm not gonna fill up my head with a bunch of bad thoughts. Believe me, I have enough bad thoughts to last for the rest of my lifetime as it is. It's all goin' to be OK. I am gonna be OK. You and Amy are gonna make a nice family and life will go on. Right? I don't wish anything bad on either of you. I wish you both nothing but happiness and a bunch of pretty little young'uns to raise. There ain't nothing to forgive. Be happy."

Laurine, always the mother and anxious to smooth out the bumps in the awkward situation, grinned big and said to them all. "Listen, we've got a big platter of fried fish and some corn maque choux in there, why don't we all go in and sit down and have us some supper?"

Pierre and Amy both answered at the same time, "We would love to, but *non*, Ms. Laurine, we can't do that, but thank you for the invitation. Maybe another time."

Pierre said, "Amy's mama probably has supper waiting for us at home, and we don't want to get on her mama's bad side." He laughed nervously and began to gently lead Amy out of the room and toward the porch. He guided her and held onto her arm as she maneuvered down the steps, ever watchful for her safety. It was obvious that they cared for each other. They left holding hands as they walked down the dirt road toward Amy's parents' house.

CHAPTER FORTY-FIVE

The Thibodauxs stood there watching until they rounded the curve and got out of sight. Then they started breathing again. Jean Marc felt a nudge against his left leg and reached down absentmindedly to scratch Chili on the head. Jacque let out a low whistle and headed inside to supper. Jean Marc followed with his mama hanging on to his arm as they walked.

"Poooyiiii, boy, I nearly fainted when I saw you come up to the dock. I was hopin' they would be gone before you got here. You got bad timing, yeah."

"No, Mama, Pierre is right, it is better to get it all out and deal with it. We have all been friends for our whole lives. We don't need any family feuds goin' on, no. You said that I'm gonna meet somebody one day who is right for me and then you will be a grandmère again. In fact, I might have already met her." He poked her gently on the arm and laughed softly as they went inside to eat.

Laurine gave him a big grin but didn't say any more. She knew that the best way to kill a budding romance for her son was for her to be too enthusiastic too early. It was better to be quiet and let him figure things out for himself. Mothers had to be particularly careful about things like that. She ought to say that she didn't like the girl. For most boys, that would be enough to cause them to be engaged within a week but then, Jean Marc was not like most boys. He was serious-minded and after being hurt once already, he would not make another move like that until he was ready. That was fine, she wanted him to take his time and be certain. Inside her heart, she was hoping that Emma was still going to be the one who mended her son's heart. She planned to ask the Blessed Mother about that again tonight when she prayed. The Blessed Mother knew a lot about sons.

She took the lids off the big black pots and ladled the hot corn dish into their bowls and added a big spoonful of white rice in the middle for the ones that wanted it. Her husband Jacque wanted everything with rice and she tried to keep him happy. That corn maque choux mixture of fresh corn and peppers and onions and other good things smelled even better today than it did when she made it last night. While the bowls were cooling, they started in on the crunchy fried fish. There was fresh brewed coffee and some sliced tomatoes out of the garden. Jean Marc ate his fill. It was good eatin' and a lot better than what he ate in the Army for sure.

"Mama," he said, "Them Army cooks didn't know the first thing about seasoning. Everything they cooked was bland. The soups they made me eat in the hospital were as dull as dishwater. I used to daydream about your cookin' all the time." He laughed and grinned at her.

His mama blushed and told him, "I am glad that you like my cookin', son, but I am not that good. You know my mama was a much better cook than me. Your Tante Zina was a better cook than me too. They both had a special touch that I can't copy. I never will know what they did that was different but theirs was always the best, I'm just saying."

Papa reached his plate for another piece of fried fish and said, "It seems awful good to me, *Sha*, and I don't think anybody ever ran away from your table, now did they? And they never went away hungry either. Your sister and your mama were both fine cooks, Laurine, but I gotta say, I like your cookin' the best." His wife blushed but was grinning from ear to ear as she put the biggest piece of fish on her husband's plate.

Jean Marc's mama was a very good cook, but then most every woman and quite a few of the men that he knew were good cooks. His own papa made the best jambalaya he ever tasted. He wondered if Emma was going to be a good cook. She was more of a city girl, so he was not sure. It didn't matter that much; he could scramble an egg if he got hungry. He was still crazy about her whether she could cook or not. He smiled to himself as he decided to ask her about her cooking skills the next time they were together.

CHAPTER
FORTY-SIX

On his way back to his own place, he thought about several things he might be tempted to ask Emma. One question kept jumping to the top of the list, but he would wait for a little longer before taking that drastic step.

And he also realized that he was bone tired and would not be likely to need any "medicine" to get to sleep tonight. Seeing Amy and Pierre and getting that hurdle out of the way had been good. He was relieved now that it was over. Another thing was strange, in a way, but now that he had Emma in his life, he did not seem to have so many "ailments." He had not had any Hadacol since the night before he met Emma. He would have to figure out another way to get his mama into Cousin Dud's Hadacol tent show, if she still wanted to go.

C

Sacam usually landed his spacecraft successfully and covered it with vines and leaves to make it as close to invisible as possible. This time was another one of those few when it didn't go smoothly. The last time he crash landed had resulted in Jean Marc's discovering his half buried aircraft in the swamp a few months before. Fortunately, he had been able to sit quietly inside the machine without being discovered and wait until Jean Marc got frustrated enough to leave the area. Then he revved up the atomic engine and managed to back it out of the muddy crater and get it moved to a better spot. His small single-seat shuttle aircraft was designed for landing on a smooth hard surface and these swamps were not even close to being smooth or hard. That was another unique feature about this part of the unusual planet. Even when he thought he had spotted a good landing area, he soon discovered the soft marshy land would sometimes partially swallow his craft once he set it down. The ground was so soft and saturated with water that it even moved when you walked on it. Other times, the trees got in the way and he often had to dodge the large puddles of water and even the animals that sometimes fouled up a landing. The large clearing that appeared to be solid grass occasionally turned out to be soft and spongy earth or even water that was covered in algae. Tonight, he thought that he had found a clear and solid landing site, but when he touched down, his aircraft slid across the thick slimy mud, hitting small woody trees and rolling end over end and bouncing off the side of a huge cypress stump before sticking itself into the mud. The nose was buried so deeply he knew that it would be a strain pulling it out this time, even with engines as powerful as those in his aircraft. He had been thrown around inside the craft and felt pretty banged up even though he was in a safety harness. His neck hurt some and there was a very sharp pain in his belly where he had hit the controls several times in his rollovers. He reached up to push a button on the top control panel and felt another sharp pain. He unhooked his safety harness and reached down to touch the painful spot. The burning sensation grew worse. Simply touching the spot with his fingers made him feel light-headed. He tried to climb out of his bucket seat and found that he was not able to stand. He began to do a quick mental assessment of his physical condition and found that things were not adding up well. He was almost certain that he had severe internal injuries even though he had no visible cuts or bumps on the outside. He carried a first aid kit, but his small kit had nothing in it to deal with such a serious injury. He called his wife on his high-powered radio and told her of his situation. She was very concerned because there were no medical facilities on this world that could help him. Their bodies were different enough that no one on Earth would know how to treat his injuries. He told her that he was fairly certain that his injuries were life threatening and they planned the way they would handle things if he was correct. She reported his accident to the proper authorities but at this point neither of them knew if a rescue ship could be dispatched or not. He also told her what a good wife she had been and that he was sorry to leave her this way. The mortal part of him was very frightened. The scientist part of him wondered what would happen. The idea of death was fascinating, but even he had to admit that it would be better if it were happening to someone else.

CHAPTER FORTY-SEVEN

At first, Sacam's wife, Meera, had not understood his wanting to come back to this remote area again so often and so soon after his last visit here. Then he had told her about the many things still left to see and collect and he also told her all about meeting the Earth being, Jean Marc Thibodaux. She wanted to see the beautiful places that Sacam described and very much wanted to meet an Earth being. She had made him tell her again that she could make a trip with him to the blue marble planet before the collecting was finished. Sacam had seemed more interested in this particular planet than in any of the others that he had ever visited before. He was also more interested in that specific part of the planet for some reason. He had talked more about it than any other place he had been. There were other scientists collecting in the colder parts of this world now but Sacam insisted on returning to this same spot. He had seen deep forests and deserts and everything in between but was amazed at this swampy area and was not nearly ready to declare it done. Every trip there, he discovered new plants or insect species. Fortunately, it was also sparsely populated, so he had felt reasonably safe from detection...except for Jean Marc.

Making trips to Earth was considered a dangerous

mission by their Galactic Exploration Department. The chance of problems was discussed at every meeting. The beings who inhabited this beautiful planet were constantly waging wars with each other and appeared to be an extremely violent breed. Experience showed there were not many Earth beings who appeared to be friendly enough to have a relationship with a person from another world. Many of them seemed to be intelligent and they were making progress in science and medicine as well as atomic energy. But even so, their first use of the new form of atomic energy was to use it in war. In all probability it would not be very long until they would be trying space travel themselves, but coming here was still considered a very dangerous mission and the explorers were cautioned over and over to stay away from the human inhabitants. Most of the committee members were afraid that Earth people would either lock them up in a zoo or kill them just to see what they looked like inside. They did the same to each other as well as to the animals who shared the world with them, so it was not at all difficult to envision them doing those things or worse to a visitor from space. Earth people were very much believed to be angry and violent. None of the committee felt confident enough to send a team there to officially greet them and offer to be friends or to exchange information.

One group also pointed out that as intelligent as the Earthlings were, they also seemed to be totally self-absorbed. They all appeared to think that their own little blue ball was the only inhabited planet in the entire universe. Such arrogance and naïve thinking was ridiculous.

CHAPTER FORTY-EIGHT

The Earth newspapers wrote about moving lights in the skies and called them UFOs...Unidentified Flying Objects. There were many sightings and many reports. Most of them had nothing to do with Sacam or his people or any other group that he knew of. He had never met anyone else from his own small planet that had made friends with a real Earthling. It made him proud. He and Meera had discussed the possibility of his being bold enough one day to write an article for his own world news service as a reference for others who may choose to come here. The truth was that he was not ready to share quite yet. There was so much work to be finished. Also, as thrilled as he was to know Jean Marc, he was breaking a rule by allowing himself to be seen. He could get into serious trouble if he announced his discoveries. It was possible that his relationship with an Earthling could encourage others of his kind to attempt it and if there were complications from that, it could become a tremendous problem. That was a lot of responsibility for one person to take upon himself.

After speaking to her husband, Meera was more than a scientist; she was also a worried wife. Sacam was stranded on Earth with his damaged aircraft and a possibly fatal injury. It would take most of three Earth days to get a committee together to decide whether to send a doctor from their world to find his present location, plus the time it took to get there. She was not certain that there was anything that could be done about the situation, but she had called their close friend who worked at the local office of Galactic Exploration anyway. She very much wanted her husband home for personal reasons, but she stressed the importance of the fact that none of their technology should be left on a distant planet to be discovered. That could change the entire cycle of a developing civilization and was against every rule of inter-galactic travel and exploration. To her way of thinking, even if they could not consider making the trip to Earth strictly to save her husband, surely they would agree that they had to retrieve that aircraft and the technology that it contained. If they moved quickly enough then it might help Sacam as well.

Sacam told her in his last transmission that if he became certain that he was dying, he would give his Earthling friend detailed instructions on how to dispose of the aircraft, but Meera was not nearly as certain as her husband that this Earth being would follow the instructions. She was afraid to trust.

The Galactic Exploration Department decided to wait and observe awhile before sending a flight down to retrieve the aircraft. They didn't want to risk discovery by sending a big ship for a rescue operation and then have it found. That hurt. That meant that there was no way that anyone was going to rescue her husband. If he was mortally wounded then he would be left to die alone on a distant planet. It seemed a cruel fate for someone who had worked so hard to obtain knowledge to pass on to future generations. There were times that living by the rules was very difficult.

It was a sad situation. It hurt and angry tears fell from her large dark eyes as she mentally dealt with and accepted the decision of the committee. She felt the deep stirring of some kind of inner rebellion wanting to rise up and demand that they do something to save her husband. She would never do that, of course. She accepted the decision of the committee as she had always been taught, but for just one moment, she wished that she had to courage to stand up and ask for more. Sacam was a good man and a good scientist. He would be missed. His work was important. He was important to her. It was difficult to accept that he would no longer be there as her husband. Her son had been notified and would be arriving soon. That would mean there would be two of them walking the floor and waiting to see what would happen. It was not going to be an easy time for either of them. There were close friends and family nearby but that didn't dull the pain of losing her mate.

CHAPTER FORTY-NINE

The past week or so had been the best in the whole four months since Jean Marc got home...well, excluding the incident with Pierre and Amy last night. If he thought about it, even that was all right. That chapter of his life was now finished and he was free to move on to whatever he was supposed to do with his life. He had a couple of ideas about that.

Emma and Jean Marc were growing closer every day, and his parents liked that idea very much. They had been extremely worried about their younger son after he came home. He had to change his dreams and start over after finding his sweetheart was no longer there for him. It had hurt for a while, but now Emma was in the picture and Jean Marc no longer looked like a brokenhearted soul. He looked downright happy.

Since he met Emma, he was standing taller and smiling again. Family friends in the village had noticed and were beginning to hope that the two youngsters were interested in more than merely dancing and having a good time. The Christmas holiday season would soon be upon them and Laurine was looking forward to it now. She felt an extra reason to celebrate this year. During the recent *boucherie*, or hog killing, the whole family had waited for the couple to make some kind of announcement, but none was made. They settled for helping to make the gratons or cracklin and *boudin*, and the rendering of gallons of lard that were put aside for use in the coming months for cooking. Some of the bigger cuts of meat were salted and seasoned with spices and then hung in the smokehouse, and some was given to those who helped, and more was cooked and eaten that day. The liver was cooked and the intestines were cleaned and used for the spicy meat and rice *boudin* sausage that they liked so much.

Jean Marc's mother had known Emma and her parents and grandmère for many years and would love to have the girl as part of her family. She truly felt that the two of them would be a good match...better than the one with Amy Benoit, for sure. She never had thought that girl was good for her boy, especially after she confessed to loving Pierre. Some things couldn't be overlooked so easily, but Jean Marc seemed to have recovered now and she was glad. Maybe Emma could heal Jean Marc's broken heart. Only time would tell.

After Amy and Pierre's visit the night before, Jean Marc had discussed the visit with his parents at the supper table, "I am even more convinced now that God knew what was best for me all along. Amy was always a nice girl, but I did not feel the same for her when I finally saw her face to face last night. My heart did not react at all the way I had expected it to when I was seeing the girl I had once believed was my only true love. It wasn't even because she was here with her husband or that she was big and pregnant. None of that would have mattered at all, if I still felt the same love that I had expected to feel. If I was still in love with her, wouldn't I have felt mad as hell? Shouldn't my heart still feel broken and full of wantin' to bust something wide open? I didn't feel any of that stuff. She just looked like a nice girl who was happily married and going to have a baby and now my heart doesn't feel broken at all anymore. God bless 'em and I hope that they are very happy. I hope that they have a whole house full of little kids. I do hope they take after Amy, 'cause Pierre, he ain't as handsome as Mr. Clark Gable, that's fer sure. He is still as scrawny as he always was. I would have figured that he'd have filled out some by now. "

They all laughed at that.

Seeing the silver flash in the sky the night before made Jean Marc expect to see his friend Sacam that day. Early the next morning, he headed out in the direction of the flash and tended to his traps, going about his business as usual, but keeping his eyes open for the little man in the silver suit. Chili chased one scent after another and seemed to be enjoying the day in his own doggy way until he caught a smell that made him snort and shake his head the way he did around Sacam. He ran through the undergrowth and bayed as if he were on a hunt. Chili's baying was the only sound Jean Marc heard. The swamp was deathly quiet again. That made the hair on the back of Jean Marc's neck stand on end. Something was wrong. He could feel it in his bones.

CHAPTER FIFTY

Jean Marc followed Chili out of curiosity and also because he still feared that the dog would try to take down an animal bigger than himself and get hurt in the process. The old dog was like a member of his family in his own way, and Jean Marc worried as much as he would over any other family member. He didn't want that old dog to take on a bear or something that could do some real damage.

As he jumped over a large puddle, he spotted the strange silver aircraft again through a break in the trees and bushes. It was stuck into the mud almost like it was the first time he saw it except that the nose was buried much deeper this time and it was jammed up against a big tree stump and sitting at an odd angle. It was also different because this time, it looked and sounded alive. The skin of the aircraft hummed and shuddered in an unusual way. Although Jean Marc was only a self-taught shade tree mechanic, who knew nothing about aircraft of any kind, especially those from other worlds, even he could tell from the noise that the machine was not functioning properly. He approached it cautiously and knocked on the metal with his knuckles.

"Sacam, it's me, Jean Marc, are you in there?" he called silently from inside his mind.

Suddenly, a clear window opened up and he could see his friend partially strapped into a form-fitted seat inside the cockpit. He did not look well at all. He slowly reached out with a long thin finger and touched another button. A doorway opened upward so that Jean Marc was able to go inside. Jean Marc knelt down to get to eye level and questioned his friend. "What happened, buddy? When you gonna learn how to land this damned thing? You need to get some of them pontoons I saw once on a plane that landed on water."

Sacam tried to smile but passed out in his seat with the straps holding him upright.

"You OK?...No, you are not OK. What can I do to help you?"

Sacam drifted in and out of consciousness. Jean Marc managed to get him out of the seat but the small man was obviously in severe pain. His face had a greenish flush and he had several large green bruises on his head and hands. Jean Marc gently laid the still figure in the bottom of the pirogue and moved back the way he had come as quickly as possible. He pushed the same button that he'd seen Sacam push and the door began to close. He jumped out before it went too far and began to examine his friend. He was very worried.

This little silver-suited man had come to mean a lot to him and he did not want to see him die either. He had seen enough death to last a lifetime and was not ready to deal with it again.

Even Chili whined as he sat in the bottom of the boat. He seemed to realize that this was a serious situation and even reached out to lick Sacam's hand.

Sacam woke up and rubbed the old dog's head and told Jean Marc, "He has never done that before." He tried to laugh but the effort made him cry out in pain and pass out again.

Chili looked back at his master with confusion in his eyes. He clearly looked to his master to fix things. Jean Marc was the master. He had to fix this.

Jean Marc's mind was racing. He wanted to fix it too, but was not coming up with any solutions.

He patted Chili's head and told him, "I am trying, boy, I am trying. Let's get him home and we will see what we can do. Maybe it is not as bad as it seems. He is a tough fellow. Remember, he survived the alligator attack." Jean Marc needed the positive thinking as much as the dog.

There was no real doctor here in Butte La Rose. The nearest medical doctor was a long and bumpy truck ride away in Lafayette. That was too far to drive with someone injured as badly as Sacam seemed to be. It would also cause quite a problem with trying to keep his spaceman friend a secret. Jacque Moreau, the local barber, had done some duty as a surgeon upon occasion when somebody got cut and needed stitching up or a broken bone set, but Sacam did not appear to have any open wounds or broken bones. There was also the fact that Jacque Moreau was the biggest gossip in town. He was worse than an old woman about telling tales and that would not do at all.

His mama was a good healer, but if he called on her, she would get the whole family involved and that was most likely not a good idea either.

The only real answer that he could come up with was to trust Emmaline with his secret. That was a scary thought, but he had to do something for Sacam. She was the nearest medical help and he could not see any other choice. This was definitely going to test the new relationship, but maybe it was better to test it now than later. He decided to get the small man to his own house as quickly as he could and then go find Emma. She was the only hope for Sacam and he would deal with her reaction after it was done.

He didn't know how he would find the words to explain things to her, but he felt that he had no choice but to try. He had to do what he could for his friend.

Jean Marc carried Sacam in his arms like a child once again, placed him on his own bed as gently as he could manage, and covered him up to his chin with a sheet and blanket to keep him as warm as he could. He told Sacam in his mind, "Please hang on, I am going for help. It will be OK. Don't worry and please don't die."

CHAPTER FIFTY-ONE

Then he ran as fast as he could with his gimpy leg. He prayed all the way to Emma's house. He pounded on her door until she answered and then managed to gasp, "Bad accident...need help...please...my friend... he is hurt inside, please, come fast. My house."

She grabbed her bag of emergency medical necessities and ran down the steps to the truck. She had the motor running before Jean Marc even finished climbing into the passenger side. He turned sideways on the bench seat and tried to find the words, but none would come out of his mouth. How do you tell someone that you have a wounded man from another planet at your house?

Emma was asking over and over, "Jean Marc, who's been hurt? What happened? Is it Boo or Elloi? Is it Aaron? I need to know what happened so I can figure out what to bring with me and what I can do to help."

By the time his breathing had calmed down enough to talk, they were there. When they reached his yard, she pulled up as close to the porch as possible. She looked at him strangely and then jumped down out of the truck and headed for the door with quick steps, leaving him behind to go at his own pace. He let her go inside and followed as fast as he could.

She was more than a little shocked when she pulled the sheets back and found the pale little man in a silver suit lying there on Jean Marc's bed with his big dark eyes wide open. She raised one eyebrow and looked at Jean Marc with major questions on her face, as he came limping through the front door. He went straight to the sink and got a clean cloth and wet it and brought it to her. He knelt down across from her and explained as simply as he could.

"Emma, this is my friend Sacam. He visits here often to collect insects and plants to study. He takes them to his world and then brings them back after he looks at them for a while. He crashed his aircraft and it appears to me that he has hurt himself pretty bad this time. Can you please see if there is anything that you can do to help him? He is a good man."

She listened carefully. Much to her credit, she didn't panic. She gently began to examine the man and was as careful as any medical doctor could ever be.

Sacam blinked his large dark eyes and reached out both hands to touch Emma's temples with his fingertips as he had done to Jean Marc when they first met. Her eyes flew open and she backed up immediately, but Jean Marc told her, "It's OK. Don't be afraid, he is not going to hurt you. He has to put his fingers on your face and then you can understand his thoughts and he can understand yours. It's like he takes in all that is in your mind or memory or something. It sounds crazy but it works. You will be able to communicate with him after that."

Sacam reached out again and this time, Emma let him touch her temples. Both men could see the surprise in her eyes when she understood his thought messages. He guided her examination and told her about the accident. She opened his silver suit and touched his pale, hairless body with gentle fingers. He winced as she probed, and Jean Marc could hear the thoughts they shared. Sacam told her that he already knew that he was most likely mortally wounded. The green tint to his skin was from internal bleeding, what she would call very large and very deep bruises. The worst injury was most likely a rupture of the organ that produces his green blood. In our human bodies, it would be called the spleen. He said he needed to have surgery to repair the injuries and a transfusion. But that was not possible here. His blood was green, he said, because of his chlorophyll-based diet. She asked if there was anything that she could do to help him and he said that he had been bleeding inside ever since the crash last night but there was none of his blood to use for transfusion here. He thanked her for her kindness and gentleness. He told them that he had already radioed home and spoken with his wife, Meera, and was prepared to pass over to whatever the Creator has planned for him next.

She asked if he was in pain. He said, "Yes, it hurts badly."

Emma dug into her bag and found a little cloth sack full of dried-up brown material. She went to the kitchen and boiled a little water and made willow-bark tea to soothe his pain. After a few minutes' steeping time, she brought a cup of the warm tea for him to sip. He drank it in spite of his rule of not tasting the products from other planets. He wanted to know the name of the plant and how she mixed the tea. He looked at Jean Marc and chuckled lightly, and told him that he liked the taste of the drink. He said that now he was actually considering the taste of things, something that he had never thought much about until Jean Marc made him aware of it. He also told them after a few minutes that the tea had indeed helped the pain. Even as he lay there dying, he was still fascinated by the wonderful bounty of useful plants found on this beautiful world. There was so much work left to do here. He was sad to be leaving it unfinished.

Sacam gave them precise instructions on how to dispose of his remains when it was over. He did not want his body or his aircraft to ever be discovered. All three of them agreed that it was extremely important that no one else on Earth know of his existence.

He also told them that he considered himself extremely fortunate to have known two Earth beings. He said that he wished that he could go home and tell his people that there are Earth beings who are not as violent as they had believed. He told them that the hands-on touch that allows them to communicate was much more than that. He said that by touching them, he had absorbed much of the knowledge that they both had in their minds. He was sad that he had learned so much from both of them and would not be able to share that knowledge with his people. Jean Marc knew about the animals and the land itself. Emma's mind was rich with the knowledge of the plants and their uses. They could have helped him finish his work. But now it appears that the Creator had other plans for him and he had no choice in the matter.

Both Emma and Jean Marc told Sacam that his instructions would all be followed exactly as he requested. He had asked Jean Marc to sink the aircraft in the deepest and most remote part of the swamp, but left the precise location up to them. Jean Marc hated to see that interesting piece of equipment be drowned in the swamp, but he understood that it had to be done.

The two of them sat with Sacam until he was unconscious. Jean Marc felt so helpless and sad. He told Emma about the time they had spent getting to know one another. He apologized for involving her, but she said that there was no reason for an apology and told him that it was an honor to be a part of this very special secret. Knowing that she felt that way about it made him feel better. He had been worried about her reaction to the situation.

She softly stroked Sacam's pale bald head and told Jean Marc that she was as fascinated as he was by the idea of knowing for sure that beings from other planets existed. She wanted to make Sacam's last hours as comfortable as she could and wished that there was more they could do for him. Perhaps the future travelers should carry a bottle of their blood in their ships.

Sacam came awake for a few minutes before he died. He thanked them both again and told them that they were the only Earth beings that he had ever known and he was sorry to leave them and even sorrier that he had to leave them with so much work to do.

Jean Marc held his friend's long and slender hand and told him once more that he had enjoyed their time together and was very sorry to lose him as a friend. He said that he understood that the things he asked for them to do were necessary and he would take care of them. He and Emma promised to do exactly as he had instructed. Sacam closed his large eyes and sighed softly and then passed away. His death was the same as any Earth person's death. The life force left his body and all that was left was the hollow shell of the pale little man inside a silver suit.

CHAPTER FIFTY-TWO

After a few moments of silent prayer, Emma and Jean Marc wrapped him in the handmade quilt from Jean Marc's bed and then moved his body to the pirogue. They made their way back to the crash site as quickly as possible. Together they carefully strapped Sacam's body into the pilot's seat of the silver aircraft as he had been when Jean Marc found him the day before. Both of them touched their friend and said prayers. They would have felt better if they had been able to bring a priest to him to give him a proper funeral. Since that was out of the question, they did the best they could. They asked The Creator to watch over the spirit of their friend from so far away. They asked the dear Lord Jesus to watch over him and make him welcome. They asked the Holy Spirit to give him peace and guidance. They asked the Blessed Mother to take this man to her heart and help him find his way in the place he now called home. They both hoped that one day they would get to see him again, wherever they all ended up. It was hard to say goodbye. Both of them were saddened by the things they had to accomplish.

They touched the button as they had been told to do and jumped out of the door as it slowly came down behind them.

Then they tied a long and heavy rope to the beautiful and curious machine and hauled it out of the mud. The rising tide had loosened it somewhat and now it moved. They floated it to the deepest and darkest part of the swamp. It was a place where the water was thick with sulfurous mud and minerals, and a rainbow film of oil floated on the surface. There was an odor of rotten eggs and a slick black ooze bubbled up from the slimy bottom. They both felt certain that there was no reason that anyone sensible would want to venture into this part of the swamp, ever. Even the trappers and hunters avoided this part of the swamp. The bubbles rose up through the dark greasy water as the machine rocked back and forth with flashes of silver barely showing through as it sank into the muddy depths. Jean Marc had to swallow back the tears as he silently said goodbye to his friend. Once again a friend had died in his presence. It was a sad day.

Neither of them had anything to say as they slowly paddled back the way they had come, preferring to mourn in their own private ways. The dark and dangerous atmosphere of that part of the swamp made the long boat ride seem even more sad and lonely. Jean Marc was grateful that Emma was there with him. It helped a little. He was still a little concerned about her reactions to his secret and hoped that they would get a chance to talk about it later. He knew that she had been greatly affected by the experience but hoped that it would not bring the end of his new dream of their making a life together. He was afraid to ask her about it right then. He needed to grieve for a little while and was not ready to take the chance of bringing even more sadness into his thoughts.

Emma and Jean Marc went back to his house and sat

at the small kitchen table and drank coffee in silence. They were both in shock over all that had happened and exhausted from the efforts of burying their friend and his airship. Neither of them knew what to say to the other. Nothing seemed to express what was in their hearts. They finally stood together with their arms around each other and cried silent tears of sadness. Jean Marc could hardly believe that they had shared this, the biggest secret of his life, and then spent most of that day on a mission to keep the secret from getting out. He was very aware that there was no other person in his life with whom he could have or even would have shared that secret. Emma was special. He knew that from the first night they met again after not seeing each other since they were children.

Jean Marc kissed the lips that he already loved so very much. He knew now that this was the woman he wanted to be his forever. She knew his secrets. She warmed his heart and gave him hope for the future. They finally did what Earthlings have done for centuries when faced with death. They reaffirmed life by making love. They kissed and touched and took comfort from each other. The warmth from their love made them forget the cold wet burial of their friend, even if it was only for a little while. Then they slept.

When they woke up in the wee hours of morning, they went out on the porch and looked up at the stars. Jean Marc could not help but look for the streak of silver in the nighttime sky.

He told her, "I am going to miss him."

Emma said, "I wish there had been more time for me to

get to know him. He seemed like a good man. He was not nearly as different as I would have expected a man from another planet to be. He was a man, wasn't he?"

"Oh yeah, he was a man. He had green blood and a funny little egg-shaped head with big eyes and a little mouth that he didn't use to talk, but yeah, he was quite a man."

They looked up at the stars and wondered which one was Sacam's home. They wondered how many more planets out there were occupied. Sacam had said he had been to many other worlds to make his collections. They wondered how many others from places out there had come to this Earth to visit. They wondered if more would come here in the future. Sacam never named any other planets being occupied by beings but he had made that one reference to the fact that his people had hidden themselves when the strangers came. Jean Marc wanted to know who the strangers were and where they had come from. But Sacam may not have wanted them to know any more than he told them.

CHAPTER
FIFTY-THREE

Jean Marc drew her fingertips up to his own lips and asked, "You do realize that we have to keep this secret to ourselves? Would you be willing to share all my secrets for the rest of our lives?" He kissed her hand.

She said, "Yes, of course. I was hoping that you would ask. I want to be here with you. I didn't want to go back to Baton Rouge. I think we did OK as a team, don't you? "

He knew for certain now that his life was changing direction again. He was confident. There would be a future for him and for Emma. They did make a good team. He could easily imagine that they would marry and make a life for themselves here in Butte La Rose. He would fish and tend his traps and she would heal the sick. They would be good together. With luck, they would have beautiful children for Mama and Papa to love and spoil. Now...finally, he felt whole again and his life had direction and purpose. They stood on the porch and watched the star-studded sky. They knew things now that other Earth people did not know. It seemed like a heavy responsibility...but they were both glad to know the truth. They also knew that the God and Creator they worshipped was indeed the God of the universe.

They both wondered what the rest of the world would say if they knew the things they knew. What would the

Church say about it? The Church would probably not like it very much. Or maybe they would want to meet the space beings so that they could convert them to the Catholic faith. The Church wanted to convert the entire world. Jean Marc could not imagine the excitement in the Vatican if they discovered there was an entire universe out there to convert. After thinking such thoughts, he felt guilty and crossed himself and said a silent prayer.

Both of them were certain that Sacam was right. Most Earth people were not ready to accept the knowledge that his kind would have been able to give them. Maybe they would be someday in the future, but not yet.

CHAPTER FIFTY-FOUR

Mama and Papa were thrilled with the news that Jean Marc and Emma were getting married. The next day the young couple drove to Baton Rouge and Jean Marc formally asked her father for his daughter's hand in marriage and was very pleased that Emma's papa said he was glad to give his permission. He had told Jean Marc that he did expect him to protect his daughter and care for her for the rest of his life. Jean Marc told him that would be an easy agreement to make. Her papa also told him that he should not go into the well to get a stray bucket again, because this time there may not be a rope handy that was long enough to get him out. They laughed about his antics as a young boy. But Mr. Hebert was glad that his Emma had found a man who truly seemed to love her. Mrs. Hebert welcomed him to the family with a fine dinner of chicken fricassee and fluffy white rice. Jean Marc was glad to note that his future mother-in-law was a very good cook. She also informed him that she had taught her daughter everything that she needed to know about the kitchen. He grinned at that. He had been meaning to ask her about her cooking skills but had forgotten all about it when he found Sacam's crash site the next morning. Maybe he wouldn't starve after all.

Jean Marc went back home to get things ready for them

to live as man and wife. Emma stayed with her parents to prepare for the wedding. Neither saw much reason for a long engagement, so they chose a date that was only a few weeks away. That left both of them with long lists of things to get done very quickly.

Emma's house was larger and she needed the space for her healing work as well as for storage of her herbs and special books. That meant that Jean Marc was going to move his meager belongings to her house except for the traps and his boats. He decided to use his grandfather's old cabin as a fishing and hunting camp even though it was only a couple of miles from his new home. It was more convenient to leave the fishing and trapping gear there than to be moving it back and forth. It only took a couple of small loads in Boo's old truck to get his moving done. Chili padded along beside him back and forth from the house to the truck as though he had to supervise each armload. Jean Marc finally realized that Chili might be thinking that he was being left behind. When he put the last box in the truck, he invited Chili to sit beside him on the ride back to Emma's house. Chili jumped up on the seat and sat as though he belonged there until the truck began to move and then he flopped his big warm body across Jean Marc's lap and hung his head and front feet out the window to watch the scenery go by. His tongue was hanging out and he drooled all over the outside of the truck's door. It was an awkward position to hold for long, so it was good that the ride was short. He laughed at the dog hanging out the window and told him, "Listen up, Chili dog...don't you go getting ideas about liking this too much. You are NOT gonna drool all over my new car when I get it. You got that?" Chili ignored him and barked out the window just because he could.

The next morning, Jean Marc sold Mr. Breaux the rest of his hides and counted the money in his coffee can. He finally had enough to do the things left on his list.

CHAPTER FIFTY-FIVE

Boo drove him to Lafayette, where he went to the jewelry store and looked at gold wedding bands. He didn't have enough for an engagement ring, but no one that they knew had one of those anyway, so it did not seem unusual. The gold band was the important part and he was able to get a nice one for Emma and another like it, only bigger, for himself. He tried his on and got a thrill when he realized that in a short time, he would be married to his beautiful Emma. The ring felt as natural as he had expected. He wanted to be a husband. He wanted to be a father.

He and Boo went to the car dealerships to find the perfect automobile to carry him and his new bride on their honeymoon and into their new life together.

Jean Marc had learned to drive Papaw's old truck as a young boy. He had sold the old truck before leaving for boot camp, which had given him a little extra money to live on until he got his first paycheck. In the Army, he drove a truck sometimes and even drove a jeep for a while during the war.

Jean Marc and Boo each drove several of the shiny new cars before finally making a decision. Boo was having a fun time driving all those new cars. He wanted to drive each one as fast as he could make it go, but Jean Marc reminded him that he didn't own the car and would most likely end up having to pay for it, if he wrecked it. That made Boo a little calmer but the whole experience gave him a huge case of New Car fever.

Jean Marc didn't take long at all to feel comfortable behind the wheel again, but for him, this was serious business. He looked at the engines and the interior and the tires of every one they saw. He even checked out a few used vehicles to see if there were any bargains out there, but finally decided that this was a new life he was beginning and he and Emma deserved a new car.

He liked the deep gray of the 1946 Packard that was on the lot. The lines were smooth and to Jean Marc, it looked like a rich man's car. Unfortunately the price was also more suited to a rich man's budget. That would have been Boo's choice, but Jean Marc had a frugal streak and could not justify the extra expense in his own mind.

He found a 1946 Ford that was still very nice and more suited to his pocketbook. The soft gray cloth of the seats was less luxurious than the leather ones in the Packard, but more practical for what he felt was a normal life in Butte La Rose, Louisiana.

He paid cash for the vehicle and was able to get the tag right there at the dealership and then they drove it back home. His teeth were shining in a big ole grin the whole way back. He headed straight for his parents' house to show off the new car.

A new automobile was a big thing in their small community. Not every family had a car. Some had trucks to drive and a few still used their mules and a wagon to carry their goods. His mama clapped her hands and jumped around with her eyes dancing with glee. She climbed into the back seat and refused to get out again until he took her for a drive. Papa got into the front passenger seat. He didn't say a lot but he rubbed his hand over the upholstery and nodded, so Jean Marc knew that he was liking it just fine. Off they went to make the rounds. They drove past the church and the General Store so that Mama could wave at her friends from the back window. She felt very grand. She and Papa had only owned pick-up trucks during their lifetime and a grand automobile like this was a big step up in stature for their family. Jean Marc couldn't remember ever seeing his mama so excited before. He told her that he would drive her around any time that she wanted to go somewhere now and she was thrilled. He even promised her that after the honeymoon was over, he and Emma would take her and Papa to Baton Rouge to see a picture show. Papa still pretended that seeing a picture show wasn't anything he cared for much but Mama clapped her hands together like a schoolgirl and grinned from ear to ear. She was already day-dreaming about a trip for shopping. She may not have a lot of money to spend nor was there anything in particular that she needed, but she was anxious to go look in the windows in the bigger stores of Lafayette and Baton Rouge. Window shopping was always an exciting thing to do.

CHAPTER FIFTY-SIX

The day of the wedding finally arrived. Jean Marc stopped by to pick up his parents and drove them to the little white church that was down the road from Emma's parents' home in Baton Rouge. Mama was dressed in her best church dress and Papa had put on his suit and a tie. He even wore his fedora. It had been a very long time since Jean Marc had seen his father in a tie. Mama talked the whole hour that it took to get there. She was excited and pleased and could not hold it all inside. Jean Marc was pretty excited, himself. He was confident that the marriage was going to be a good one and he was also looking forward to their honeymoon trip to New Orleans. There had not been any engraved invitations mailed out, so the invitations were done in person and by word of mouth. No one had been certain of how many of their neighbors would be there.

The pump organ played softly as the Thibodaux family was seated in the church to await the marriage of their younger son. They could not help but look around. The church was beautiful with its hand-carved woodwork and statues of Jesus and his Blessed Mother and saints all around. The smell of cypress wood, beeswax, and incense made them feel reverent and very much at peace.

They began to see familiar faces from home. Aaron and his wife, Patrice, and their children came. The Landry family was well represented too. And the Boudreauxs and the Comeauxs and lots of Heberts. Even the Fontenots and Berthelots were there. There were Thibodauxs and Aucoins and it seemed to Jean Marc that half of his small community was seated in this church to see him wed. It gave him a warm feeling inside. He had not expected so much support. He thought that it might be that the outpouring of support was as much for his parents as for him. That made sense to him and he accepted the idea completely. He might have gone off to fight in an unpopular war, but his parents were loved in Butte la Rose.

The ceremony was simple and made even more special by the fact that Father Rodriguez had known Emma since he baptized her as an infant and was also the one who offered her First Communion. He looked on the young couple with love and well wishes in his voice and in his heart.

After the ceremony, Papa declared that he thought the priest made the knot pretty tight. Mama said that Emma was the most beautiful bride that she had ever seen. Jean Marc had to agree with that. They all danced at the wedding party later and ate plenty of delicious food. The wedding was a little more formal than the outdoor ceremony they had attended for cousin Marguerite but was exciting and beautiful and looked and felt like a fairy tale wedding to his parents. They had the reception outside under the shade of oak trees that were older than anyone attending. Jean Marc thought it was a bit like a fairy tale too when he took his bride into his arms and danced their first dance as man and wife. He remembered the dance he shared with the bride at his cousin's wedding and thought that this was much different. This lovely young woman in his arms was his alone and he was happier than ever before in his life. He wished that Sacam could be here to see another real Cajun wedding. Somehow he got the feeling that he was there in spirit. He could hear Sacam's voice in his mind, telling him to be happy.

When the festivities began to die down, Jean Marc loaded his new wife's luggage into their new automobile and the two of them got ready to leave for a weekend in New Orleans for their honeymoon. Crazy Boo Landry and Elloi Comeaux had tied old shoes and tin cans to the car and somehow fastened a big sign on the trunk lid that read "JUST MARRIED." Jean Marc had told them not to do any of that, but of course, they didn't listen. "That is what best friends are for," Elloi told him. Now they would either have to stop somewhere and take off all that clutter, or drive the whole way to New Orleans with horns honking at them and people waving to them as they went by. They decided to leave the stuff tied on and enjoy the brief spell of notoriety. It would be fun. How many times would they get to be newlyweds?

Papa had agreed to drive Emma's truck back home so that it would be there when they returned from their trip. It also gave his parents a way to get back to Butte la Rose.

CHAPTER FIFTY-SEVEN

The happy couple got to New Orleans late that night. The valet took their luggage in and told them he would park their car in the hotel parking garage. They felt very special to be waited on that way. The bellman then took their luggage and escorted them to their room. He left them alone to face their first night together as Mr. and Mrs. Jean Marc Thibodaux. It was pretty special.

Even though he had always enjoyed making love to Emma, he was pleased to find that their lovemaking was even better when they were married. He felt certain now that they belonged together and would stay this way for as long as they both lived.

The next day they rode on the Mississippi riverboat and enjoyed beignets and café au lait at the Café du Monde. They went inside the Cathedral to pray and light a candle for Sacam. They looked at the sidewalk artists and watched a juggler put on a show and enjoyed a wonderful dinner at a fine restaurant. Then they went back to their hotel and enjoyed a glass of wine before retiring. Emma thought that her honeymoon was something right out of a movie script. Jean Marc laughed to himself as he thought that all that was missing was Rochester to bring them a refill for their glasses. It was the most elegant trip that either of them had ever imagined. Sharing it was a wonderful beginning for their marriage, full of love and hope and dreams for a happy future.

Jean Marc allowed himself a few minutes to think about how disappointed he had been a few months ago when he came home and discovered that Amy was married and not to be his wife at all. Now he realized that God must have known that something better was right around the corner... or in his case, right down the road. He was so glad that Amy was happily married and now, he was going to be happy too.

Reality set in as the happy couple came back to their home and settled into the community just as they had hoped to do. Jean Marc tended his traps and fished and hunted as he always did. On weekends they would sometimes sleep at the cabin for the fun of it. They ate most Sunday dinners with Jean Marc's parents and visited with Emma's folks at least once a month in Baton Rouge. Emma worked her healing talents on all the local residents and was becoming well known as a *treateur* as good as Tante Nettie. She began to collect her own chickens and piglets that were brought to her as payment for her services. She read through all of Grandmère's notebooks and found recipes for new creams and ointments and tried them all on Jean Marc and herself, so that she could be familiar with them before giving them to those who sought her services. They picked blackberries and made jam that they put up into glass canning jars. They planted a garden that was growing more each day. Life as a married couple was exactly as both of them had hoped that it would be. All that they were missing was the patter of little feet and they were both confident that it would happen in God's own time.

CHAPTER
FIFTY-EIGHT

Boo and Elloi both took jobs with an oil company and began spending much of their time away from home. Boo's family missed him terribly and though the money was good, none of them were happy with all the separation. Jean Marc had considered taking the same kind of job but was more comfortable doing his hunting and fishing. He sold his alligator hides and furs and with the extra income from Emma's work, they got along very well on what they had. He also acted as a guide for hunting parties who wanted to hunt in the woods and swamp. He had already spent enough time away from home and was not anxious to leave again. His life was full and he and Emma were content. The Sheriff was making retirement plans and tried to recruit Jean Marc to run for the office in a couple of years. The Sheriff pointed out that Jean Marc's military service would qualify him for the job and Jean Marc finally told him that he would consider it. He didn't want to be Sheriff, but since Butte La Rose was a place where crime was almost unheard of, he figured that it would be an easy job. The extra income would be nice and it would not change his lifestyle much at all.

Emma even managed to convince Jean Marc that bankers were not going to steal his money and that having it in the bank was safer than keeping his cash in a coffee can hidden under the woodbox. Now they had a savings account that drew interest and were saving for a new bedroom suite that had all matching pieces. They saw exactly what they wanted in the Sears & Roebuck's catalog that Mr. Landry had at the General Store. Once they had the amount of money that they needed, they would order the furniture from the catalog and it would be delivered straight to their home in a big truck.

Their only worrisome thoughts concerned a certain silvery aircraft that was buried in the deepest part of the swamp and the fact that the oilmen seemed awfully interested in that exact location. Boo came home one weekend all excited because he had heard the oil company bosses talking about drilling some test wells in the Atchafalaya Basin. He hoped that if his company started drilling in their own swamp, then he would not be away from home nearly as much, and he and Marie were both praying that it would happen. Jean Marc and Emma were not as pleased by the news. They were concerned with having the drilling in their own area and what it would do to the wildlife there, but even more concerned about secrets that could be uncovered if full-scale drilling did start. They asked Boo to try to find out more about it. Boo thought it was because Jean Marc might be interested in the job. He told Jean Marc that the work was very hard but that the money was good. He didn't like being away from home so much but he liked the fact that he also now had a bank account and was less worried about the future of his family.

A few weeks later he came over and told Jean Marc that

he had heard that the oil company had already done the exploration in the swamp for drilling sites and noticed the rainbow sheen on the surface of the water. Their company had gotten the leases from the government that included that big section of land and water down in the stinky part of the swamp. They had already made the arrangements to bring in the heavy equipment for a test well.

Unfortunately, Boo had been told that he was not going to get to work on the test well. He was to stay on the rig where he was already working. He was not happy about that. But he had recently gotten a raise and decided that he was not going to complain too much. Marie was already spending the pay raise in her mind. Marie wanted an automobile and with three children, he was thinking it would be nice to be able to drive them all around. With the old pickup he always had to leave a couple of the kids at home with Grandma. When they all got a few years older the whole family would not fit into the truck at all anymore unless he started hauling them in the back with the cargo. The older ones loved to do that already but it was not good when it started to rain.

With more automobiles on the roads, all over the country, the demand for oil and gasoline had grown tremendously even in the short time since the end of the war. The swamps of south Louisiana were full of promising sites for drilling. With luck, there would be a real strike and this area would become a part of the blossoming oil boom.

The oilman who was taking measurements out in the swamp smiled as he allowed his dream of "the big one" to rest in his mind for a second. He looked down in the depths of the water and thought he saw a silver flash but dismissed the flash as some kind of trash that had been dumped out here. Dumping had always been a problem in swamps and wooded areas. His crew would clean it all out when they got here to drill the well.

He began to shout orders to the men who were moving the drilling equipment into place. There were cypress trees to be cut down and huge cypress stumps to be removed as well as massive marine pilings to be driven deep into the floor of the swamp for the platforms that had to be built to hold the drilling equipment. It was a dirty job but one that he loved, and he was ready to see what there was to find out there in this God-forsaken place. Those strong odors might be nasty smelling to some folks, he mused, but to him it smelled like Money. He needed a strike right then. He had invested his own money and all that he could borrow in this well. He was convinced that he was going to find a gusher here.

CHAPTER FIFTY-NINE

The colored lights were turned off in layers beginning at the top, after the huge silver flying machine landed in a clearing that Sacam had described meticulously in his notes. Meera stood in the open doorway and looked around. It was exactly as her husband had described it, right down to the sounds and the peculiar odors. A great white heron lifted his wings and flew past her, making her gasp with pleasure. Sacam was right. This was a special place. She cautiously walked down the ramp and followed a well-worn path to a wooden building nearby. She recognized it as Jean Marc Thibodaux's home, again from her husband's descriptions and from her study of his notes. It was a strange-looking rustic structure made from rough sawn cypress boards. The roof was rusty metal. The windows were small with glass panes. There was wood smoke coming from a pipe that stuck out the side of the wall. Homes on her planet were neat and clean with a lot of metal and cement. This was fascinating but did not look much like a place that she would want to spend too much time. The wood smoke was irritating to her eyes.

Meera stood at the door of the strange dwelling that sat up on high pilings at the edge of the water. She was not certain of the protocol involved in entering an Earth being's dwelling. She raised her hand to push on the opening but before she touched the wood, Emma opened the door. The two stood there for a moment and Emma stammered, "... Sacam?"

Her hand flew to her heart with shock. She turned to find Jean Marc standing behind her. His mouth was opening and closing with the same shock that she was feeling. Meera blinked her large eyes and stepped closer to the two Earthlings. She reached out her long slim fingers to touch Jean Marc's temples and took in all his thoughts and language in a few seconds' time. Then she turned to Emma and did the same. Now they could all share thoughts. They gazed at her and asked why she was here.

Meera explained, "I am Meera. I am the mate or wife of Sacam, in your words. There are things happening in the swamp. There are workmen who are digging deep holes into the Earth to collect the black tarry substance that is used for energy here on this planet. They have started to drill one of these deep wells in the area where Sacam's ship is buried. We have come here to collect the ship and take my husband's remains back home."

Jean Marc told her, "Yeah, we were also very worried about the possibility of his ship being found. We didn't know how to reach you. What can we do to help?"

Meera told them that she had come to them only because she wanted to meet the two of them. "My husband liked you so much, Jean Marc. He spoke to me often about the time you spent together and the things that you discussed. I hope that you do not mind my curiosity. I wanted to meet you."

She nodded her head to him almost like a bow and he found himself saying, "Thank you. I have missed him very much. I can't look into the night sky without wishing that I could see the silver flash of light from his ship. I often see things that I wish I could share with him. It has been very difficult."

Meera asked them, "Would you like to come with me to the spot and be with me when we raise the ship from the water?"

They both nodded and invited her in to wait a short time while they got ready. Meera stood in the front room of the tiny cabin and looked at the rough boards that made the walls and the worn but comfortable looking furniture that filled the front room. She saw the wood stove that took up a lot of space in the kitchen and the plywood counter-tops. There was a small white table with two chairs that served as an eating area. It was so very different from what she saw every day at home. She was amazed. It felt comfortable and the longer she took in the feelings of the place, the more she liked it.

CHAPTER SIXTY

Emma and Jean Marc dressed quickly in their old fishing clothes with high rubber boots and then followed Meera a short distance back into the swamp, where she had left her large cargo salvage ship and a crew of men who were ready to haul Sacam and his smaller aircraft out of the mud. Emma and Jean Marc were also amazed at the things they saw. Sacam had told them that his people were all very similar in size and in their look. There must have been at least twenty crewmen with Meera and they all looked exactly the same to Emma and Jean Marc. They all were about four feet tall and they all had the same features. They all wore silver uniforms exactly like the one that Sacam had worn. There were labels and insignia on some like a uniform, but overall, it was very confusing to Jean Marc and Emma. The voices they heard inside their heads were high pitched and spoke a totally foreign language. Meera was the only one they were able to understand and the only one that understood them. The rest sounded like a chorus of squeaks and clicking noises, unlike any language either of them had ever heard.

The small people seemed to be highly skilled and efficient at their various jobs. But while they were all running around like little silver ants, it was impossible for Emma and Jean Marc to tell one silver suit from another.

Meera invited the two Earth beings to come aboard her

ship and then strapped each of them into a small but rea-sonably comfortable seat. Meera helped them to get the seats adjusted to fit their larger bodies as much as possible. The huge metal doors slid down with very little sound and closed securely as the lights danced across the control panels and the engine began to purr softly. The aircraft was tremendous but made so little noise that they were able to relax and talk to each other in their normal speaking voices. It was glorious. The huge craft rose slowly and began to move forward above the tree line. Meera asked them if they wanted to see out the windows. They both nodded their heads excitedly. She touched a tiny spot on the wall and a large clear window appeared. They saw the cypress trees below them and the dark water glowed with phosphores-cence as they passed over it. They held hands and stared with wide eyes as the scenery changed beneath them. The swamp was a beautiful place from ground level, but even more so from this high vantage point. The flocks of water birds lifted off and flew beside them and one looked them in the eyes as he flapped his wings harder trying to keep up. He was quickly left behind. Their swampy paradise was the most beautiful sight that either could have imagined.

When they reached the spot where they had sunk the ship containing Sacam's remains, they were both shocked to see a huge number of lights glowing so brightly that it was almost like daylight. There were men in rough clothes and hard hats working on a large wooden platform holding machinery that pounded huge marine pilings deep into the floor of the swamp. The constant pounding noises and the whine of the machinery were deafening. Meera pressed another button and a very fine mist of some kind sprayed out of their aircraft to cover the men who were staring up at the huge aircraft. Meera explained that it was a harmless plant-based mist that would cause the men to forget what they had seen.

"We hate to resort to drugging the beings working there, but we have noticed that they are working all through your Earth days and nights. There does not seem to be a time when there is no one in the area. Our office of the Galactic Exploration Department has been watching. The work crews moved in quickly and have gotten this much activity going in a very short time. We wasted two of your Earth day and night periods watching to see if they would leave this place unattended but they are bringing in more equipment and more men every day. So we decided that it was necessary to do this thing immediately. I hope that this has not caused you too much distress. The mist will not harm them in any way. I give you my word. We cannot have them reporting our presence to anyone. I am sure that you understand.

My husband spoke of you so favorably. He had even told me that I would get to make a trip here to meet you myself one day. I do wish that we had made the trip together. I took a very big risk bringing you here tonight. I do hope that you will understand that it is extremely important that none of the rest of the beings here find out about my husband or our visits to this world of yours. We have determined that most of the beings here are not yet ready for a meaningful relationship with others of our kind. We have seen too much violence and lack of tolerance in most Earth beings. Perhaps one day we will be able to meet openly, but for the moment, we feel strongly that it is best to keep the visits hidden."

Both Jean Marc and Emma assured her that they understood completely and would never mention any part of the secret to anyone. Meera smiled and nodded her head.

The huge aircraft hovered over the part of the swamp where the remains of Sacam and his ship lay buried in the mud. The humming sound gradually changed pitch and got louder and a circle of very bright lights shined downward from beneath the belly of the aircraft. A large square panel slid to one side and left an equally large opening in the floor of the loading dock. The humming sound grew louder and the water beneath them started to churn and bubble, stirring up all kinds of debris from the bottom. After a moment or so, they saw a flash of dull silver under the dark-colored water as the powerful magnetic rays pulled the smaller aircraft upward through the muck. Finally Sacam's ship broke the surface and was towed magnetically into the cargo bay, dripping with muddy water and raining leaves and sticks and sludge. It settled into a docking space on the roof of the room where Meera and her guests stood watching the procedure. A group of large spray nozzles came down from the ceiling and sent strong jets of water over the entire surface of the ship to wash away as much debris and whatever Earth creatures might still be attached to the vehicle as possible. The muddy water fell back into the swamp.

Emma wiped the tears away from her eyes and cheeks and held onto Jean Marc's hand while Meera led them out of that room as the docking door slid back across the large opening. The magnetic ray stopped its humming noise and then another loud buzzing sound assaulted their ears. Meera handed them each a pair of ear covers and explained that they had to bathe the ship in a disinfectant ray to rid it of bacteria. She told them that because this planet has a lot of smaller life forms like bacteria that could possibly prove deadly to their species, there wasn't any choice. They peeked through a small opening in the door as bright green and purple lights swept over the entire ship. There were pinging sounds as well as loud zaps and sizzles as the light found and destroyed the tiniest bacteria and algae that had hitched a ride on the unusual vehicle. As soon as the disinfection process was finished, Meera opened the door to the room again so that they could enter. They all gasped at the horrible stench. The ship was covered in a dried pattern of boiled mud.

CHAPTER SIXTY-ONE

Meera pressed her thin right hand on the side of the ship and closed her large eyes for a moment. Emma was not able to read her thoughts that were in her own language, but the emotion was easy enough to read. She was about to lay eyes on the body of her dead husband and it was bound to be a painful moment. Emma reached out and touched Meera's hand and they clasped fingers for a time. They looked into each other's eyes and Jean Marc thought to himself as he watched, "A loving wife is a loving wife, no matter where she is from." The door slid upwards and there he was sitting in the padded seat reclining exactly as they had left him. Well, his bones were there anyway. His flesh was gone, long since decayed. His egg-shaped skull was there with the large empty eye sockets. His hands were spread across his abdomen exactly as they had placed them. Meera gently touched his skull and closed her eyes again in a moment of silent longing. It was very sad to see. As soon as they had all reassured themselves that nothing was amiss, they backed out of the aircraft and closed the sliding door again.

The three of them went back to the seating area and sat down to each digest the scene in their own way. In a few short moments, Meera stood and walked forward to the cockpit of the large aircraft and began to make preparations to take off again. She closed the cargo doors and flipped switches and pressed the colored buttons. She looked very efficient and in control as she adjusted the soft hum of the engines and brightness of the lights and once again raised the ship up above the activity below. The oilfield workers appeared to be as busy as ever and were paying no attention at all to the large silver ship above them or the things that they had done. When the ship reached the correct altitude, it sprayed out another fine mist of the herbal drugs that caused the men to forget.

Meera said, "Tomorrow they will not remember what they have seen or done. Losing the memory of this time will likely be confusing for them, but we hope that they will blame it on their being tired from not getting enough sleep. That seems to be a very physical job. It would be no surprise if they were tired. If things were different, we could show them how to create energy without all that labor, but I am afraid that such knowledge in the wrong hands causes more problems than it solves. We have seen it happen on other worlds. It is far better to let each world figure things out in their own way." The ship began to move across the swamp with almost no sound at all.

Jean Marc thought to himself, *Well, that answers one question. Evidently there are other worlds out there that are inhabited. It seems that Meera is not as skilled as Sacam at hiding the secrets.*

In a few minutes they found themselves back at the place where they had gotten on board. They walked down the ramps to the familiar ground beneath their feet and turned to say their goodbyes to Meera.

She touched Jean Marc on the arm and told him in his mind, "Thank you for being such a good friend to my husband. It meant a lot to him and that means a lot to me. I am very glad to have met the two of you, though I have to admit that I wish it had been under different circumstances. Sacam enjoyed his visits to this place so much. It is so completely different from our world. He brought me thousands of notes and what your world calls photographs of specimens to study. I have boxes of plant material and water samples as well as air samples and a few carcasses of dead animals that he found. It will take a very long time to process them all. I hope that I will be very well rewarded for the work I will do."

Then she turned to Emma and said, "You were very kind to Sacam as well. I know from reading your thoughts that you tried to save him. He knew that he was dying and I am sure that he was very grateful to have the two of you with him at that time. Dying alone on a strange planet would be difficult for anyone. You made his passing much easier I am sure. As a wife, I appreciate that."

Each of them told her how glad that they were to have gotten to meet her and how much it meant to them to witness the recovery of Sacam and his ship. They told her that they were relieved to know that he was not stranded here on this world any longer, and was going home now. It seemed right and proper. They both hoped that she would come to visit again one day.

Meera said that she seriously doubted that she would ever get to come here again but that she would think of them both often. "There will be others of our kind, but they will most likely continue to avoid the inhabitants as they always have before."

Meera put out her hand to shake hands in what she had learned was a normal human gesture of friendship. Emma used that hand to pull Meera into an old-fashioned Earthly hug. Meera got tears in her eyes as they parted. She was beginning to understand even more about her husband's fascination with this planet and its inhabitants.

Emma and Jean Marc promised again to keep the secret. Meera smiled and said she had complete faith in them. She told them to be sure to stay and watch the take-off and that she would wave goodbye as they left. She said that the sight of the large ship taking off would be very exciting. The young couple smiled and watched her go aboard and then stood there holding onto each other as they waited to see the aircraft lift off. They both felt certain that this was a sight that few other Earth people had ever witnessed. The whole event was fascinating. It had been a very special gift. It was certainly very exciting for them both. The engines began to hum softly and the lights began to blink on and off and change colors from white to green and back again. There were red lights on one side and green on the other, like the Earthly port and starboard. They hadn't expected that similarity, but there it was reminding them that even the universe was not as large as they once believed. It was beautiful to think of all the similarities they had discovered between themselves and their friends from another world. It was amazing that a ship so large made so little noise. Jean Marc could not help but think about his friend, Sacam, and wish that he had not passed away and that he and his family could have learned even more from each other.

The ship began to rise slowly and shortly before it moved forward, a very fine mist completely enveloped the two of them as they stood beneath the aircraft. Meera looked out and waved as the large aircraft swept across the sky.

The two Earthlings looked with soft eyes at each other and then looked up at the night sky full of stars.

"My baby girl, I am tired," Jean Marc said. "This seems to have been a very long day. I think I am ready to call it a night. Aaron said something about us taking him to Lafayette to look at automobiles on Saturday. Patrice says that she wants a car like yours to drive instead of driving the old truck like the others in the family. We Thibodauxs are moving up in the world, huh?"

Jean Marc wiped the misty rain from his face and continued, "He said that if I can go with him, he would like to go early. We'll go in his truck and then he can drive the new car home after he finishes with whatever else he wants to do over there. I will go with him myself, if you don't have any shopping to do. I know that he is wantin' to go look at some fightin' chickens that ole man Privat is trying to sell. I told him that if Privat is selling them, they're likely to be good for nothin' but gumbo, but he wants to see what he has to offer. He said for me to be ready to go by six in the mornin'. I hope he is not planning to bring those chickens home in his new car. Surely he wouldn't do that. I am thinking that means that I will be da one unloading chickens out da truck before I can come home. If you need me to pick up anything at the store, just make me a list. Are you wet, my baby? I didn't realize it was raining. Come on, *Sha*, let's get into the house and get ourselves ready for bed. I can't remember doing anything that would make me so tired, but I guess it won't hurt either one of us none to get some extra sleep."

Emma turned and walked with him through the door. She was more than ready to go to bed herself. She had to admit that she was a little more tired than usual, but she had attributed that fatigue to the new little secret that she was waiting to share with her husband. Their first anniversary was coming up in a few days and she planned to tell him then. She knew in her heart that he would be pleased.